"Where am I… room is mine?" Gabriella asked.

She could practically feel Max's incredulous stare zinging down the phone line! He let a full thirty seconds of silence elapse before replying. "I thought the whole idea here is to convince your parents we're still happily married, despite what the tabloids say."

"It is."

"Then which room do you suppose, Gabriella?"

She muttered, "The master suite?"

"Bingo! Any *more* questions?"

Indeed yes! But nothing would persuade her to come right out and ask, *Will we be sharing the same bed?*

She'd find out the answer to that soon enough!

Legally wed,
Great together in bed,
But he's never said...
"I love you."

They're...

The series where marriages are made in haste...
and love comes later...

Look out for more Wedlocked! books—
coming soon in Harlequin Presents®!

# Catherine Spencer

## THE MILLIONAIRE'S MARRIAGE

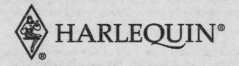

### HARLEQUIN®

TORONTO • NEW YORK • LONDON
AMSTERDAM • PARIS • SYDNEY • HAMBURG
STOCKHOLM • ATHENS • TOKYO • MILAN • MADRID
PRAGUE • WARSAW • BUDAPEST • AUCKLAND

ISBN 0-373-12220-9

THE MILLIONAIRE'S MARRIAGE

First North American Publication 2001.

Visit us at www.eHarlequin.com

Printed in U.S.A.

# CHAPTER ONE

"I'VE left word that you're expected. If I'm not home when you arrive, the concierge will let you in."

The words themselves were chillingly neutral but, even after all this time and despite everything, Max's husky baritone still had the power to make her break out in goose bumps. Holding the phone away from her mouth so that he couldn't hear how ragged her breathing had become, Gabriella fought the urge to beg him to be there himself to greet her and, matching his tone the best way she knew how, said, "Is it still Howard?"

"I'm surprised you remember, given the number of doormen who must have crossed your path in the last two years."

He made it sound as if she earned a living paying illicit visits to married men's hotel rooms! "There are few things about my life with you that I've forgotten, Max," she said stiffly. "Howard was one of the more pleasant aspects. It will be nice to see him again and know there's at least one friendly face in the building—unless, of course, you've poisoned his mind against me."

"Hardly," her estranged husband replied. "Your name rarely comes up in conversation, and then only in passing."

Though there was little doubt he was being his usual brutally direct self, even more regrettable was the fact that the truth should hurt so much. "Are you quite sure we can pull this off?" she said. "Two weeks of facing each other across the table at mealtimes might not be a long time in the cosmic scheme of things, but I suspect it'll seem an eternity when it comes to living them second by second.''

''I can manage it, if you can. And I have no doubt that you can. It will be, after all, a lot like your life—a charade. And let's face it, Gabriella, you've always shown a talent for pretending. No doubt that explains your phenomenal latter-day success as a model. How else do all those glossy fashion magazines feature you as dewy virgin bride one day, sultry seductress the next, and beach bunny yet another?''

She'd made up her mind she wouldn't get drawn into the retaliation game, no matter how he might try to provoke her, but his scornful dismissal of the success she'd worked so hard to achieve spurred her to respond, ''Why, Max, I had no idea you followed my career so closely!''

''I don't,'' he said crushingly, ''but I'd have to be brain dead not to recognize that, technically at least, I'm married to the most famous face in North America and possibly the world. Given your unquestionable versatility when it comes to make-believe, plus the fact that you're an accomplished liar, I'm sure you can pull off the image of contented wife for a couple of weeks, especially since you have so much at stake and I plan to make myself as scarce as possible most of the time. All it'll take is a little civility in public, a few harmless demonstrations of affection. We've been married over two years, Gabriella. Your parents aren't going to expect us to act like besotted honeymooners.''

''Which is just as well, since a honeymoon's one thing I've never had the pleasure of experiencing.''

But she knew about heartbreak, and loneliness, and rejection. She knew how it felt to be a bride standing beside a groom who, when he looked at her at all, did so with a blank indifference touched with loathing. She knew what it was like to lie alone in the big marriage bed while her husband slept in the guest room—a pain only slightly less unbearable than the few times when primitive need had driven him to come silently to her in the night then, when his hunger was appeased, just as silently leave her again.

She knew what it was like to be married to a man who hated her all the more because, once in a very rare while, he couldn't resist her.

"Gabriella? Did you hear what I just said?"

Startled by his unabashed impatience, she jerked her attention back to the present. "Um…not exactly."

"I asked what time they land in Vancouver."

*They:* her aged parents who thought their only surviving child was blissfully happy with the grandson of a man they revered more than God! What if they saw past the subterfuge so carefully constructed for their benefit? What if her world-famous smile cracked, and she couldn't disguise the misery?

Suddenly, when it was too late to change anything, she wondered why she'd ever encouraged them to leave their native Hungary and visit Canada, or why she thought she could pull off such a monumental deception. "Three o'clock tomorrow."

"And you're in Los Angeles now?"

"Yes. I stayed with a friend last night but I'm flying out at ten. I expect to be at the penthouse by early afternoon."

"That should leave you enough time to unpack and reacquaint yourself with the place. And while I think of it, you might want to pick up a few supplies. The stuff in the refrigerator's pretty basic and unlikely to measure up to your gourmet standards."

Why did he do that? she wondered. Why imply that she

was impossible to please and needlessly extravagant? Whatever else she'd contributed to the failure of their marriage, overspending his money was not on the list, for all that he'd been convinced his bank account was what had made her chase him to the altar.

But taking issue with him now would lead only to more acrimony and she already had enough to handle. "Grocery shopping's at the top of my list of things to do," she said, then waited, hoping he'd volunteer the information she most needed to learn, and so spare her having to be the one to raise a topic he surely hadn't overlooked.

Once again, though, he disappointed her and with obvious relief said, "I guess that's it, then. If I don't see you today, I'll catch up with you tomorrow at breakfast."

"Before you go, Max…"

"Now what?" There it was again, the weary impatience she so easily inspired in him.

"Where am I… I mean…um, which room is…mine?"

So clearly taken aback by the question that she could practically *feel* his incredulous stare zinging down the phone line, he let a full thirty seconds of silence elapse before replying, "I thought the whole idea here is to convince your parents we're still happily married, despite what the tabloids say."

"It is."

"Then which room do you suppose, Gabriella?"

Feeling like a none-too-bright child being asked to put two and two together and come up with four, she muttered, "The master suite?"

"Bingo! And since all my stuff fits easily into one closet, I hope you're bringing enough clothes to fill the other, unless you want it to be patently obvious that, like your parents, you're merely visiting. I don't imagine, given your extensive wardrobe, that's a problem?"

"None at all," she said, recovering a trace of the haughty composure that had made her an overnight sensation as a model. "I have three large suitcases packed and waiting."

"I'm delighted to hear it. Any *more* questions?"

Indeed yes! But nothing would persuade her to come right out and ask, *Will we be sharing the same bed?*

She'd find out the answer to that soon enough!

She'd grown up in a palace—a small one, to be sure, and rather shabby around the edges, but a palace nonetheless. The Tokyo apartment she'd bought eighteen months ago, when she left Max, was small but exquisite. Her most recent acquisition, a house with a lovely little walled garden on the outskirts of Rome, was a gem of seventeenth-century elegance.

Still, as she stepped out of the private elevator on the twenty-first floor and stood under the hand-painted dome in the vestibule, the magnificence of Max's two-story penthouse took her breath away, just as it had the first time she'd set foot on its hand-set marble floor.

Leaving her luggage and the sacks of groceries in the foyer, she crossed the vast living room to the right of the winding staircase and slid back the glass doors to the terrace. Tubs of bougainvillea, hibiscus and tibouchina in full flower lent splashes of exotic color to the sprawling rooftop garden. Yellow roses climbed up the south wall. A miniature clematis with flowers the size of bumblebees rambled along the deep eaves. The raised swimming pool and hot tub shimmered in the drowsy heat of the late June afternoon. People who didn't know her real reason for taking up residence here again could be forgiven for thinking she'd entered paradise.

Beyond the parapet, the Vancouver skyline showed itself off in all its summer glory. Sunlight bounced off the glass walls of newly built office towers. Sailboats drifted on the calm waters of Georgia Strait. The graceful arc of the Lion's Gate Bridge rose from the green expanse of Stanley Park to span the First Narrows as far as the North Shore where snow-kissed mountain tips reared up against the deep blue sky.

It had been just such a day that she'd come here as a bride, with the air so hot and still that the tears she couldn't keep in check had dried on her cheeks almost as fast as they'd fallen. She'd been married all of forty-eight hours, and already knew how deeply her husband resented her. She'd stood in this very spot, long after sunset, and prayed for the hundredth time that she could make him love her. Or, if that was asking too much, that she could stop loving him.

Her prayers had gone unanswered on both counts, and remembering the weeks which had followed left her misty-eyed all over again.

Annoyed to find herself so soon falling back into old, bad habits, she gave herself a mental shake and returned to the cool, high-ceilinged living room. Like the city, it, too, had undergone some change, not by new additions but by the complete removal of anything that might have reminded Max of her.

"Do what you like with it. I don't care," he'd flung at her when, as a bride, she'd suggested softening the austerity of the decor with various wedding gifts and dowry items she'd brought with her from Hungary—lovely things like the antique tulip lamp, hunting prints and painted wall clock handed down from her grandparents, and the brass trivets and finely stitched linens from her godmother, all of which she'd left behind when she fled the marriage.

Now, the cherrywood accent pieces Max had chosen before he met her provided the only contrast to the oyster-white couches, carpets, walls and deep, carved moldings. Even the classic fireplace, swept scrupulously clean of ashes, looked incapable of warmth. He had erased every trace of her from his home as thoroughly as he'd erased her from his life and, while some might admire the severe elegance of the room, without the reminders of her childhood home and family, Gabriella found it cold and hostile.

Surely, he hadn't thrown away those treasures her family had managed to save from the ravages of the political upheaval which had reduced so many once-wealthy families to poverty? Surely, as she went about the business of—how was it he'd put it, when they'd spoken on the phone that morning?—*reacquainting* herself with her former home, she'd find they'd just been stashed away somewhere?

Returning to the foyer, she averted her gaze from the stairs which led to the bedrooms, and carried the grocery bags to the equally barren-looking kitchen. Max's claim that he had only basic supplies in stock had been, she shortly discovered, a masterpiece of understatement. Although the temperature-controlled wine cellar at one end of the room was well stocked, the refrigerator contained nothing but beer, a very old block of cheese, and a carton of grapefruit juice.

Apart from a couple of boxes of cereal and some canned soup, the lower cupboards were bare. The glass-fronted upper cabinets stood completely empty, the panes staring back at her like sightless eyes. Neither cup nor plate graced their shelves.

The copper-bottomed pots and pans hanging from a stainless-steel rack above the work island were linked by a fine network of cobwebs, giving testament to how infrequently they'd been taken down. As for the built-in range and double-wall ovens imported from France, Gabriella doubted either had been used since the last time she'd cooked dinner there, over eighteen months ago.

In fact, the entire main floor of the penthouse had the look of a showpiece owned by a man who stopped by only occasionally to check on his investment, and she had no reason to suppose the upstairs rooms would be any different. There was none of the casual clutter, no sense of the warmth that speaks of a home shared by a couple in love. Her father might be fooled into believing otherwise but, as things presently stood, her mother wouldn't be taken in for a minute.

Realizing she had a host of shopping still to do, she searched through the drawers for a notepad on which to list the items needed. She didn't find one. Instead, she came across a flowered apron with a ruffle around its hem, and a half-empty tube of hand cream.

The sight caused her stomach to plummet and left her feeling slightly sick. Neither had ever belonged to her and she couldn't imagine any circumstance which would have persuaded Max to make use of them—in which case, who had?

*Don't do this to yourself, Gabriella,* the voice of reason scolded. *It's going to be difficult enough to preserve your parents' peace of mind by letting them think your marriage is on solid ground so get on with the job at hand, because it's going to take you the rest of today to make the place look lived in.*

By nine that evening, her manicure was ruined but the transformation she'd effected throughout most of the rooms was worth every chip in her nail enamel.

The pantry and refrigerator fairly bulged at the seams

with delicacies. In the storage room under the stairs, she found boxes containing the missing heirlooms; also the Herend china she'd brought with her as a bride stowed alongside crates of wedding gift crystal and other reminders of her brief sojourn as lady of the penthouse.

Now, the china and elegant stemware and goblets were again on display in the glass-fronted upper cabinets. A pretty blue bowl filled with oranges, lemons and limes sat on the granite counter beside the brass trivets polished to a blinding shine. A braid of garlic hung next to the freshly washed copper-bottomed cookware, and pots of basil and oregano nestled in a wicker planter on the windowsill.

On a shelf at the very back of the storage room, she discovered the large, silver-framed formal portrait of her and Max on their wedding day. Surprised and grateful that he hadn't tossed it in the garbage, she'd dusted it off and set it on a side table in the living room, next to two small framed photographs she'd thought to bring with her, of her parents and the brother who'd died six years before she was born.

A fringed shawl she'd found in a bazaar in Indonesia lay draped across the back of one of the couches, its bronze and gold threadwork glowing like fire against the oyster-white upholstery. Flower arrangements blazed with color on the writing desk and sofa table, and filled the empty hearth.

She'd placed slender ivory tapers in the heavy Swarovski candlesticks on the dining room table. The antique sterling coffee service bequeathed to her by her great-aunt Zsuzsanna shone splendidly on the sideboard in whose top drawers lay the freshly ironed hand-worked linens.

Upstairs, the guest room and adjoining bathroom were prepared, with lavender sachets hanging in the closet, a vase of roses on the dresser, soaps and lotions arranged on the marble deck of the soaker tub. Monogrammed towels hung ready for use, the mirrors sparkled. Crisp percale linens covered the bed—that same bed where she'd found Max on their first night as husband and wife in North America.

She'd have thought the enormous emotional toll entailed in facing *that* room would have inured her to entering the other; the one in which she'd slept—and wept—for nearly six months before she'd found the courage to walk away from her loveless marriage. Yet, with the cool mauve light of dusk pooling around her, she found herself hesitating outside the door of the master suite, a clammy dew of apprehension pebbling her skin.

She was disgusted with herself. In view of everything she'd achieved since her marriage had fallen apart, how foolish of her now to fear four walls! *Things* could not hurt her. Only people had the power to do that—and even then, only if she let them.

Surely she'd laid those old ghosts to rest? And surely...*surely*...safeguarding her heart was a lesson she'd learned well since the last time Max had trampled all over it?

Still, she quaked inwardly as she pushed at the heavy door. It swung open in smooth, expensive silence, just as it used to do when, a lifetime ago, he'd paid those brief, late-night visits to her bed.

Inside the room, filmy floor-length curtains billowed in the evening breeze at the tall open windows. Avoiding the hulking mass of the bed itself, her gaze flitted instead from the bench at its foot where one of Max's ties and a paperback mystery lay, to a pair of his shoes sprawled crookedly next to a chair, and from there to a navy golf

shirt and three wooden golf tees tossed carelessly on top
of a chest of drawers.

It was a man's room; a room so devoid of a feminine
presence that it might never have accommodated a bride.
And yet the ghosts of yesterday sprang out at her from
every corner, clamoring to be acknowledged.

Her first night there, she'd bathed in scented water, put
on the gauzy peignoir trimmed with French lace that was
part of her trousseau, sprayed a little perfume at her wrists
and throat, and brushed her pale blond hair to satin
smoothness against her shoulders. And waited for Max.

The sky had grown pearly with a new dawn before
she'd finally accepted that he was not going to join her.
And so, silly creature that she'd been then, she'd gone
looking for him. And found him spread-eagled on the bed
in the room across the hall, sleeping soundly with a sheet
half covering him from the waist down.

For the longest time, she'd simply looked at him, bewitched all over again by his masculine beauty. Such skin,
polished to bronze, such perfect symmetry of form, such
sleek, honed strength!

Oh, how she'd ached to be enfolded in his arms, to be
possessed by him! How she'd longed to feel his mouth
on hers, claiming her soul; to hear his voice at her ear,
hoarse with passion!

Driven by hunger and need and hope, she'd traced her
fingertip along the curve of his eyebrow, smoothed her
hand lightly over his dark hair. Made bold by the fact that
he didn't stir, she'd bent down to lay her mouth on his
when, suddenly, his eyes had shot open.

Instantly awake, suspicious, annoyed, he'd growled,
"What the devil do you think you're doing?"

"Isn't it obvious?" she'd whispered, hoping the

warmth of her lips against his would ignite an answering fire in him.

Instead, he'd turned his face away so that her kiss missed its mark and landed on his cheek.

"Don't," she'd begged. "Please don't turn away from me. I need you, Max."

She might as well have appealed to a slab of stone for all the response she evoked. Ignoring her completely, he'd continued staring at the wall, and even all these months later, she grew hot with embarrassment at what had followed.

She'd pulled back the sheet and touched him—tentatively at first—beginning at his shoulders and continuing the length of his torso until she found the sleep-warm flesh between his thighs.

"It doesn't prove a thing, you know," he'd informed her with quiet fury when, despite himself, he'd grown hard against her hand. "It's a purely reflexive response— any woman could bring it about."

"But I'm not just any woman, Max. I'm your wife," she'd reminded him. "And I love you. Please let me show you how much."

And before he had time to realize her intention, she'd let her mouth slide over the muscled planes of his chest to his belly and then, with a daring born wholly of desperation, closed her lips softly over the silken tip of his manhood.

His breathing had quickened. He'd knotted his fingers in her hair and tried unsuccessfully to stifle a groan. Sensing victory, she'd slipped out of his hold and the peignoir in one swift move, and aligned her naked body, inch for inch, against his.

She'd seen the corded tension in his neck, tasted the film of sweat on his upper lip when he'd grudgingly let her turn his face to meet hers and succumbed to the sweeping caress of her tongue over the seam of his mouth.

She'd known a glorious tremor of expectation when, unable to hold out any longer, he'd hauled her to sit astride him and braced her so that, with the merest surge of his hips, he was buried inside her, tight and powerful. She'd felt the muscled flex of his abdomen, the steely strength of his thighs. Seen the rapid rise and fall of his chest.

He'd spanned her waist, framed the curve of her hips, drawn a line from her navel to her pubic bone, and then farther still, until he found the one tiny spot in her body most vulnerable to his measured seduction.

Sensation had engulfed her and left her body vibrating, from the tips of her toes to her scalp. Such pleasure! Such exquisite torture! She'd yearned toward him, wanting to prolong the delight only he could bring, but encroaching passion had slammed down with such vengeance that neither of them had been able to withstand it.

Caught in a maelstrom of emotion sharpened to dazzling brilliance by the spasms ravaging her body, she'd sensed her eyes growing heavy, slumberous almost. But his had remained wide open. Unblinking. Unmoved. As though to say, *You might wreak havoc with my body, but you'll never sway my heart or mind.*

"Satisfied?" he'd said, when it was over. And, with that brief, indifferent question, managed to degrade their union to something so cheap and unlovely that she'd cringed.

Twenty-four months should have been time enough to lessen the hurt. A sensible woman would have forgotten it altogether. But she'd never been sensible where Max was concerned and if the tears scalding her cheeks now weren't proof enough of that, the dull, cold emptiness inside where once she'd known warmth and life and passion, should have been.

What would it take, she wondered, to cure her of Max Logan and heal the scars inflicted by her marriage? Would there ever come a time that she'd learn to love another man as she still loved him—and if so, would she love more wisely the next time?

Although dense silence greeted him when he stepped inside the penthouse, he knew at once that she was there. Quite apart from her suitcases still parked by the front door, and the scent of flowers everywhere, as well as a host of other clues that she'd made herself thoroughly at home, the atmosphere was different. Vibrant, electric, and unsettling as hell. A forewarning of trouble to come.

Dropping his briefcase on the desk in his office—one area, he was glad to see, that she hadn't tried to camouflage into something out of a happy homemaker magazine—he made a quick circuit through the rooms on the main floor before climbing the stairs. The thick carpet masked his footsteps thoroughly enough that she was completely unaware of him coming to a halt at the entrance to the master suite.

Shoving his hands in his pockets, he leaned against the door frame and watched her. She stood at the highboy dresser and appeared to be mopping her face with his golf shirt. But what struck him most forcibly was how thin she'd become. Not that she'd ever been fat or even close to it but, where once she'd been sweetly curved, she was now all sharp, elegant angles, at least from the rear. Her hips were narrow as a boy's, her waist matchstick slender.

Though probably a prerequisite for all successful fashion models, it wasn't a look that appealed to him. Even less did he like the air of fragility that went with this underfed version of the hellion he'd been coerced into marrying. It edged her too close to vulnerable, and once he started thinking along those lines, he was in trouble, as he very well knew from past experience.

"I'd appreciate it if you'd wipe your nose on something other than a piece of my clothing," he said, relishing how his voice suddenly breaking the silence almost had her jumping out of her skin.

But when she spun around, the expression on her face made short work of his moment of malicious pleasure. He'd forgotten how truly beautiful she was. In particular, he'd forgotten the impact of her incredible eyes and, suddenly, he was the one struggling for composure as memories of the night they'd first met in her father's house rushed back to haunt him.

"I'd like you to meet my daughter," Zoltan Siklossy had said, as footsteps approached along the flagstone path that ran the width of the front of the rambling old mausoleum of a place.

Max had turned and been transfixed, the impact of the city skyline beyond the Danube forgotten. Backlit by the late May sunset, she'd appeared touched with gold all over, from her pale hair to her honey-tinted skin. Only her eyes had been different, a startlingly light aquamarine, one moment more green than blue, and the next, the other way around.

Fringed with long, curling lashes and glowing with the fire of priceless jewels, they'd inspected him. He'd stared back, mesmerized, and said the first thing that came to mind. "I didn't know Magyars were blond. Somehow, I expected you'd all be dark."

A stupid, thoughtless remark which showed him for the ignorant foreigner he was, but she hadn't taken offence. Instead, she'd come forward and laughed as she took his hand. "Some of us are. But we Hungarians have a mixed ancestry and I, like many others in my country, favor our Finnish heritage."

Though accented, her English was perfect, thanks, he later discovered, to an aunt who'd studied in London years before. Her laughter hung like music in the still, warm evening. Her hand remained in his, light and cool. "Welcome to Budapest, Mr. Logan," she purred. "I hope you'll allow me to introduce you to our beautiful city."

"I'm counting on it," he'd replied, bowled over by her easy self-assurance. Although she looked no more than eighteen, he believed her when she told him she was twenty-seven. Why not? After all, her parents were well into their seventies.

In fact, she'd been just twenty-two and the most conniving creature he'd ever met—not something likely to have changed, he reminded himself now, even if she did look about ready to keel over in a dead faint at being caught off guard.

"I'm not wiping my nose," she whispered shakily, clutching the shirt to her breasts.

He strolled further into the room. "What were you doing, then? Sniffing to find evidence of another woman's perfume? Checking for lipstick stains?"

Something flared in her eyes. Guilt? Shame? Anger? "Should I be? Do you entertain many women here, Max, now that I'm no longer underfoot all the time?"

"If I do, that's certainly none of your business, my dear."

"As long as we're married—"

"You left the marriage."

"But I'm still your wife and whether or not you like it, you're still my husband."

He circled her slowly and noticed that her eyes were

suspiciously red-rimmed. "A fact which apparently causes you some grief. Have you been crying, Gabriella?"

"No," she said, even as a fresh flood of tears welled up and turned her irises to sparkling turquoise.

"You used to be a better liar. What happened? Not had enough practice lately?"

"I…" Battling for composure, she pressed slender fingers to her mouth.

Irked to find his mood dangerously inclining toward sympathy, he made a big production of tipping the loose change from his pockets onto the shelf of his mahogany valet stand. "Yes? Spit it out, whatever it is. After everything else we've been through, I'm sure I can take it."

Her voice, husky and uncertain, barely made it across the distance separating them. "I hoped we wouldn't…be like this with one another, Max. I hoped we'd be able to…"

She swallowed audibly and dribbled into another tremulous silence.

"What?" He swung back to face her, stoking the slow anger her distress threatened to extinguish. "Pick up where we left off? And exactly where was that, Gabriella? At each other's throats, as I recall!"

"I was hoping we could get past that. I think we *must,* if we're to convince my parents they need have no worries about me." She held out both hands in appeal. "I know you…hate me, Max, but for their sake, won't you please try to remember there was once a time when we liked each other and, for the next two weeks, focus on that instead?"

# CHAPTER TWO

HER reminder touched a nerve. They *had* liked each other, in the beginning. He'd been dazzled by her effervescence, her zest for life. Only later had he come to see them for what they really were: a cover-up designed to hide her more devious objectives.

"My father treats me as if I were made of bone china," she'd confided, the day she took him on a walking tour on the Buda side of the Danube, some three weeks after he'd arrived in Hungary. "He thinks I need to be protected."

"Not surprising, surely?" he'd said. "You've had a very sheltered upbringing."

She'd batted her eyelashes provocatively. "But I'm a woman of the world now, Max, and quite able to look out for myself."

Later that afternoon though, when they'd run into some people she knew and been persuaded to join them for refreshments at a sidewalk café near Fishermen's Bastion, Max had seen why Zoltan Siklossy might be concerned. Although she made one glass of wine last the whole hour they were together, Gabriella's so-called friends—social-climbing opportunists, from what he'd observed—ordered round after round and showed no qualms about leaving her to pick up the tab when they finally moved on.

"Let me," Max had said, reaching for the bill.

"No, please! I can afford it," she'd replied. "And it's my pleasure to do so."

But he'd insisted. "Humor me, Gabriella. I'm one of

those dull, old-fashioned North Americans who thinks the man should pay.''

*"Dull?"* She'd turned her stunning sea-green eyes on him and he'd found himself drowning in their translucent depths. ''I find you rather wonderful.''

For a moment, he'd thought he caught a glimpse of something fragile beneath her vivacity. A wistful innocence almost, that belied her frequent implicit reference to previous lovers. It was gone so quickly that he decided he must have imagined it, but the impression, brief though it was, found its way through his defenses and touched him in ways he hadn't anticipated.

If she were anyone else and his sole reason for visiting Hungary had been a summer of fun in the sun, he'd have found her hard to resist. But there was no place in his plans for a serious involvement, and he hoped he had enough class not to engage in a sexual fling with his hosts' daughter.

The way Gabriella had studied him suggested she knew full well the thoughts chasing through his mind, and was determined to change them. Her usual worldly mask firmly in place again, she asked in a voice husky with promise, ''Do you like to dance, Max?''

''I can manage a two-step without crippling my partner,'' he said, half bewitched by her brazen flirting and half annoyed to find himself responding to it despite what his conscience was telling him.

''Would you like to dance with me?''

''Here?'' He'd glance at the hulking shadow of Mátyás Church, and the sunny square next to it, filled with camera-toting tourists. ''I don't think so, thanks!''

''Of course not *here!*'' She'd laughed and he was once again reminded of music, of wind chimes swaying in a summer breeze. Good sense be damned, he'd found himself gazing at her heart-shaped face with its perfect strawberry-ripe, cupid's-bow mouth and wondering how she would taste if he were to kiss her.

"My parents would like to throw a party for you," she went on, drawing his gaze down by crossing her long, lovely legs so that the hem of her skirt, short enough to begin with, rode a couple of inches farther up her thigh. "They hold your family in such esteem, as I'm sure you know. Your grandfather is a legend in this city."

"He took a few photographs." Max had shrugged, as much to dispel the enchantment she was weaving as to dispute her claim. "No big deal. That was how he earned a living."

"For the people of Budapest, he was a hero. He braved imprisonment to record our history when most men with his diplomatic immunity would have made their escape. As his grandson, you are our honored guest and it's our privilege to treat you accordingly."

"I'm here on business, Gabriella, not to make the social scene," he reminded her. "It was never my intention to impose on your family for more than an hour or two, just long enough to pay my respects. That your parents insisted I stay in their home when I had a perfectly good hotel room reserved—"

"Charles Logan's grandson stay in a hotel?" Her laughter had flowed over him again beguilingly. Her fingers grazed his forearm and lingered at his wrist, gently shackling him. "Out of the question! Neither my mother nor my father would allow such a thing. You're to stay with us as long as, and whenever, you're in Budapest"

A completely illogical prickle of foreboding had tracked the length of his spine and despite the bright hot sun, he'd felt a sudden chill. "I don't anticipate many return visits. Once I've concluded the terms and conditions of the property I'm interested in buying and have the necessary permits approved, I'll turn the entire restoration process over to my project manager and head back home.''

''All the more reason for us to entertain you royally while we have the chance then,'' she'd said, leaning forward so that, without having to try too hard, he was able to glimpse the lightly tanned cleavage revealed by the low neck of her summer dress. She hadn't been wearing a bra.

Responding to so shameless an invitation had been his first in a long line of mistakes that came to a head about a month later when the promised party took place. It seemed to him that half the population of Budapest showed up for the event and while he lost track of names almost immediately, everyone appeared to know not only of his grandfather but, surprisingly, of him, his purchase of the dilapidated old building across the river, and his plans to turn it into yet another of his chain of small, international luxury hotels.

''You see,'' Gabriella had cooed in his ear, slipping her hand under his elbow and leaning close enough for the sunlit scent of her pale gold hair to cloud his senses, ''it's not just Charles Logan's grandson they've come to meet. You're a celebrity in your own right, Max.''

She looked exquisite in a sleeveless flame-pink dress made all the more dramatic by its simple, fitted lines. The eye of every man in the place was drawn to her, and his had been no exception. ''I'm surprised people don't resent a foreigner snapping up their real estate,'' he'd said, tearing his gaze away and concentrating instead on the bubbles rising in his glass of champagne.

''You're creating work for people, bringing tourism here in greater numbers, helping to rebuild our economy.

What possible reason could anyone have to resent such a man?''

He'd been flattered, no doubt about it. What man wouldn't have been, with a roomful of Budapest's social elite smiling benignly at him and a stunningly beautiful woman hanging on his every word?

He should have been satisfied with that. Instead, he'd gone along with it when she'd monopolized him on the dance floor because hey, he was passing through town only, so what harm was there in letting her snuggle just a bit too close? Not until it was too late to change things had he seen that in being her passive conspirator, he'd contributed to the evening ending in a disaster that kept on going from bad to worse.

"*Didn't* we, Max?"

Glad to escape memories guaranteed to unleash nothing but shame and resentment, he stared at the too thin woman facing him; the woman who, despite the fact that they lived hundreds of miles apart and hadn't spent a night under the same roof in eighteen months, was still technically his wife. "Didn't we what?"

"Like each other, at one time. Very much, in fact."

"*At one time,* Gabriella, and *they* are the operative words," he said, steeling himself against the look of naked hope on her face. "As far as I'm concerned, everything changed after that party you coerced your parents into hosting."

"You're never going to forgive me for what I did that night, are you? Nothing I can say or do will ever convince you that I never intended to trap you into marriage."

"No. You stooped to the lowest kind of deceit when you let me believe you'd had previous lovers."

"I never actually said that."

"You implied it, more than once."

"You were a sophisticated, worldly North American and I wanted to impress you—be like the kind of women I thought you admired, instead of a dowdy Hungarian virgin who hadn't the first idea how to please a man."

"My kind of woman wouldn't have behaved like a tramp."

"I was desperate, Max—desperately in love with you. And foolish enough to think that giving myself to you might make you love me back." She bit her lip and fiddled with the thin gold chain on her wrist; the same gold chain she'd worn when she'd come sneaking through the darkened halls and let herself into his room while everyone else slept, himself included. "Your time in Budapest was coming to an end. You were making plans to return to Canada, and I couldn't bear the thought of never seeing you again."

"So you made sure you wouldn't have to by adding lies on top of lies."

She flushed but her gaze, locked with his, didn't waver. "No. When I told you I was pregnant, I believed it to be true."

"How convenient that the ink had barely dried on the marriage certificate before you discovered otherwise."

She gave a long drawn-out sigh. "Oh, Max, what's the point of rehashing the past like this? You don't need to spell it out for me again. I already know how you feel."

"You can't begin to know how I feel," he practically snarled, self-disgust sweeping over him afresh at the memory of how the night of the party had ended. Bad enough that he'd been duped into making love to a novice without the final humiliation of opening his door to hustle her back to her own room and coming face-to-face with her father.

"I thought I heard a noise and came to investigate,"

Zoltan had said, his voice trembling with suppressed anger at the sight of his guest standing there in a pair of briefs, and his daughter wearing a transparent negligee that showed off every detail of her anatomy. They couldn't have looked more guilty if they'd been caught stark naked! "I had no idea...*this*...is what I'd find."

Over the years, Max had made his share of mistakes, but none had filled him with the shame flooding over him that night. For the first time in his life, he hadn't been able to look another man in the eye.

"You could have told my father what really happened," Gabriella said now. "You didn't have to leave him with the impression that you'd lured me to your bed."

"Do you really think that would have made him feel any better, when the damage had been done already? His beloved child had been deflowered by a man he'd welcomed into his home and treated like a son. He thought the sun rose and set on you. Still does. What was to be gained by letting him know you'd come to my room uninvited? Why the devil would I have wanted to add to his misery by telling him that?"

"If it makes any difference at all, Max, he knew I was as much to blame as you, and he forgave both of us long ago."

"But I haven't forgiven myself. And I sure as hell haven't forgiven you."

She sank down on the bench at the foot of the bed, and he saw that the slump to her shoulders was not, as he'd first assumed, that she was dejected so much as utterly exhausted. "Then why did you agree to our pretending we're happily married?"

"Because I owe it to him. He's eighty-one years old, his health is failing, and I refuse to send him to his grave a day earlier than necessary by letting him in on the true state of our relationship.''

"He might be old, but he's not blind. If you're going to curl your lip in contempt every time you look at me, and recoil from any sort of physical contact, he'll figure out for himself within twenty-four hours of getting here that we're a long way from living in wedded bliss. And my mother won't take a tenth that long to arrive at the same conclusion.''

"What are you suggesting, my dear?" he inquired scornfully. "That in order to continue bamboozling them, we practice married intimacy by holding an undress rehearsal tonight?''

Color rode up her neck, a pale apricot tint so delicious it almost made his mouth water. "We don't have to go quite that far, but would it be such a bad idea to practice being civil to one another?''

"Depends on your definition of 'civil.'''

"I won't initiate sex when you're not looking, if that's what's worrying you, Max. Subjecting myself to your outright rejection no longer holds any appeal for me.''

"I'd be more inclined to take that assurance seriously if we were occupying separate beds.''

He waited for the reproaches to follow, a variation on her old theme of *You don't even try to understand how I feel,* followed by a crying spell. Instead, she stood up and faced him, her spine poker-straight and her expression uncharacteristically flat. "I won't dignify that remark by trying to refute it. Believe whatever you like, do whatever you like. For myself, I haven't eaten since early this morning, so I'm going downstairs to fix myself a light supper.''

"You look as if you haven't eaten in a month or more, if you ask me,'' he shot back, irked by her snooty attitude. He wasn't used to being blown off like that, nor was he about to put up with it. "And if how you look now is what being stylishly thin's all about, give me good, old-fashioned chubby any day of the week."

"I can't imagine why you'd care how I look, Max, and I'm certainly not fool enough to think your remark stems from concerns about my health." She brushed a surprisingly badly manicured hand over her outfit, a cotton blouse and skirt which whispered alluringly over silky underthings. "What you apparently aren't able to accept is that what you prefer in a woman is immaterial. I'd like it better if we could be cordial with each other because it's a lot less wearing than being disagreeable. But you need to accept the fact that I'm long past the stage where your approval is of the slightest consequence to me."

If she'd slapped him, he couldn't have been more stunned. The Gabriella he used to know would have turned cartwheels through downtown Vancouver during the afternoon rush hour, if she'd thought it would please him. "But you still need me, Gabriella," he reminded her. "Why else are you here?"

"Only for the next two weeks. After that, I'll be as happy to leave you to wallow in your own misery as you'll be to see me go."

Well, hell! Baffled, he shook his head as she stalked out of the room. This new, underfed edition of the woman he'd married didn't believe in mincing her words—or give a flying fig about anything he might say or do as long as he didn't blow her cover during her parents' visit.

On the surface at least, a lot more than just her dress size had changed since she'd entered the world of international fashion. Unless it was just another act put on solely for his benefit, his wife appeared to have developed a little backbone since she'd flounced out of his life within six months of forcing her way into it!

\*     \*     \*

She was shaking inside, her composure on the verge of collapse. Perhaps it was the cruel irony of the setting: the big marriage bed, so invitingly close they could have tumbled onto the mattress together in a matter of seconds if the mood had taken them, juxtaposed beside her finely tuned awareness of his unabashed animosity. Or perhaps it was as simple as his having shown up unexpectedly and taken her by surprise. In any event, she had to get away from him before she burst into tears of pure frustration.

Given that he'd acted as if she was the last person he wanted to spend time with, she didn't expect him to follow her downstairs, but he showed up in the kitchen about five minutes later to announce, "I've taken your luggage up to the bedroom."

"I could have managed it on my own, but thank you anyway," she said, laying out the French bread, cold barbecued chicken, olives, heart of palm salad, and mango salsa she'd purchased at the gourmet deli down the street.

He ambled over to inspect the food. "That chicken looks pretty good."

"Are you hinting you'd like some?" She pulled a chef's knife and fork from the wooden cutlery block next to the countertop cook surface and slid the chicken from its foil-lined bag to a cutting board.

"If you're offering, yes. Thanks." He helped himself to an olive and cast an appraising eye over the changes she'd made in the kitchen. "You've been busy. This place almost looks lived in."

Choosing her words carefully because, although she itched to ask him who owned the apron and hand lotion, she wasn't about to give him another opportunity to tell her to mind her own business, she said, "It had a somewhat unused look, I thought."

"Because I'd stored all the china and stuff you left

behind, you mean? Not everyone appreciates fine things, Gabriella, and knowing how you value yours and would eventually want to reclaim them, it seemed best not to leave them where they might get damaged.''

She managed an offhand shrug. ''But you were always very careful with them...unless, of course, you're referring to...other people?''

''What you're really asking is if I ever let another *woman* loose in here.'' He removed two of the wineglasses she'd arranged in the upper cabinet, then strolled behind her to the refrigerator. She heard him rummaging among its contents, and the clink of a bottle tapping the edge of a shelf before he swung the door closed. ''Well, as it happens, I did. For about a month, beginning the week after you left.''

Hearing him confirm her worst fears shocked Gabriella into betraying the kind of distress she'd sworn she'd never let him witness in her again. ''You mean to say you didn't even wait until the sheets had grown cold before you let another woman into my bed?'' she squeaked, and refusing to vent her outrage where it truly belonged—on him!— she accosted the hapless chicken, wielding the knife with savage intent. ''Why doesn't that surprise me, I wonder?''

''I didn't say that.'' Calmly, he rummaged in one of the drawers for a corkscrew.

''Not in so many words, perhaps, but the implication is clear enough! And so is the evidence!'' Brandishing the two-pronged fork, she gestured at the drawer. *That* drawer! ''I saw what's in there, so don't bother denying it.''

He laughed. ''And what is it that you saw, my dear? A body?''

''Don't you dare laugh at me!'' Hearing her voice threatening to soar to top C, she made a concerted effort to wrestle herself under control. "I found the apron and the hand lotion."

"Well, as long as you didn't also find high heels and panty hose, at least you don't need to worry you're married to a cross-dresser."

"*Worry? About you?*" she fairly screeched, aiming such a wild blow at the chicken carcass that a wing detached itself and slid crazily across the counter. "Let me assure you, Max Logan, that I can find better things to occupy my mind!"

Suddenly, shockingly, he was touching her, coming from behind to close one hand hard around her wrist, while the other firmly removed the knife from her grasp and placed it a safe distance away. "Keep that up and you'll be hacking your fingers off next."

"As if you'd care!"

"As a matter of fact, I would. I don't fancy little bits of you accidentally winding up on my plate."

"You heartless, insensitive *ape!*" She spun around, the dismay she'd fought so hard to suppress fomenting into blinding rage. "This is all one huge joke to you, isn't it? You don't care one iota about the hurt you inflict on others with your careless words."

"It's the hurt you were about to inflict on yourself that concerns me." As if he were the most domesticated husband on the face of the earth, he pushed her aside and started carving the chicken. "You're already worried your parents might guess we're not exactly nuts about each another, without your showing up at the airport tomorrow bandaged from stem to stern and giving them extra cause for concern."

"Don't exaggerate. I'm perfectly competent in a kitchen, as you very well know."

He jerked his head at the unopened bottle of Pouilly Fuissé. "Then make yourself useful and uncork that."

"Do it yourself," she snapped, the thought of how quickly he'd taken up with someone else once she'd vacated the scene rankling unbearably. *She* had honored her wedding vows. Why couldn't he have done the same?

"Now who's being unnecessarily hostile?"

She detected marked amusement in his voice. Deciding it was safest to keep her hands busy with something harmless lest she forgot herself so far as to take a meat cleaver to him, she began preparing a tray with plates, cutlery and serviettes. "At least," she said, "I haven't given you grounds for divorce."

"There are some who'd say a wife walking out on her husband is ample grounds for terminating a marriage."

"Then why haven't you taken steps to end ours?"

Finished with the chicken, he turned his attention to the wine. "Because we agreed there was no pressing need to formalize matters, especially given your parents' age, health and religious convictions." He angled a hooded glance her way. "Unless, of course, you've found some urgent reason...?"

"*I'm* not the one who went out shopping for a replacement within a week and had the bad taste to leave his possessions lying around for you to find!"

"Neither am I, Gabriella," he said mildly, his mood improving markedly as hers continued to deteriorate. "The woman you perceive to be such a threat was a fifty-nine-year-old housekeeper I hired to come in on a daily basis to keep the place clean and prepare my meals. The arrangement came to an end by mutual agreement after one month because there wasn't enough to keep her busy and she was a lousy cook. She must have left some of her stuff behind by mistake."

Feeling utterly foolish, Gabriella muttered, "Why didn't you say so in the first place?"

"Because you immediately assumed the worst before I had the chance to explain anything. Now that we've cleared up the misunderstanding, though, I suggest you take that pout off your face, smile for a change, and join me in a toast." He passed a glass of wine to her and lifted the other mockingly. "Here's to us, my dear wife. May your parents be taken in by appearances as easily as you are, and go home convinced their daughter and son-in-law are living in matrimonial clover!"

Twenty minutes later, they sat at the glass-topped patio table on the west side of the terrace. The Pouilly Fuissé stood neck-deep in a silver wine cooler. A hurricane lamp flickered in a sconce on the wall.

Outwardly, they might have been any of a hundred contented couples enjoying the mild, calm evening. Inwardly, however, Gabriella was a mess. Poking her fork into her barely touched meal, she finally braved the question which had been buzzing around in her mind like an angry wasp from the moment he'd misled her into thinking his housekeeper had been a lover. "Have you really never...been with another woman, Max? Since me, I mean?"

"Why don't you look at me when you ask that?" he replied in a hard voice.

*Because,* she could have told him, if she'd dared, *it hurts too much. You're too beautiful, too sexy, too... everything except what I most want you to be, which is* mine.

"Gabriella?"

Gathering her courage, she lifted her head and took stock of him, feature by feature. He leaned back in his chair, returning the favor with equal frankness, his eyes a dark, direct blue, his gaze steady.

His hair gleamed black as the Danube on a starless night. His skin glowed deep amber against the stark white of his shirt. He shifted one elbow, a slight movement only, but enough to draw attention to the width of his chest and the sculpted line of his shoulders.

Miserably, she acknowledged that everything about him was perfect—and most assuredly not hers to enjoy. She knew that as well as she knew her own name. Devouring him with her eyes brought her nothing but hopeless regret for what once might have been, and painful longing for something that now never could be.

Nonetheless, she forced herself to maintain her steady gaze and say serenely, "Well, I'm looking, Max, so why don't you answer the question? Have you been with anyone else?"

He compressed his gorgeous mouth. Just briefly, his gaze flickered. "You want me to tell you I've lived like a monk since you ran off to pursue a career?"

"I want you to tell me the truth."

He shook his head and stared out to where the last faint show of color from the sunset stained the sea a pale papaya-orange. "No, you don't, Gabriella. As I recall, you're not on very good terms with honesty and I doubt you'd know how to handle it in this instance."

She flinched, his reply shooting straight to her heart like a splinter of glass. Normally the most brutally candid man she'd ever met, his evasion amounted to nothing but an admission of guilt delivered as kindly as he knew how.

Unbidden, the night she'd lost her virginity rose up to haunt her, most particularly the exquisite pleasure he'd given her after he'd recovered from the shock of finding her in his bed and before he realized her duplicity. How practiced he'd been in the art of lovemaking; how knowing and generous and patient. And most of all, how passionate!

Had she really supposed all that masculine virility had lain dormant during her absence, or that he'd feel obligated to honor wedding promises he'd made under duress?

If she had, then she was a fool. Because what right had she to expect either when he'd never professed to love her? When she hadn't a reason in the world to think he might have missed her after she walked out on a marriage which had been a travesty from the start?

But the truth that hurt the most was the realization of how easy it would be to fall under his spell again. His tacit admission that there'd been another woman—possibly even women—was the only thing which pulled her back from the brink. Another minute, a different answer, and she'd have bared her soul to him!

Staggered by her near self-betrayal, she murmured shakily, "I see."

"I suspect not," he said, "but the real question is, does it matter to you, one way or the other?"

"Not in the slightest," she lied, the glass sliver driving deeper into her heart and shattering into a million arrows of pain.

"Should I take your indifference to mean there've been other men in your life?"

"No," she said forthrightly, unwilling to add further deceit to a heap already grown too heavy to bear. "I've never once been unfaithful, nor even tempted."

"Not even by those pretty plastic consorts you team up with in your photo shoots?"

"Certainly not."

He hefted the bottle from the cooler and splashed more wine in their glasses. "Why should I believe you?"

"Because I'm telling the truth."

A mirthless smile played over his mouth. "The way you were when you told me you were pregnant? The way you were when you intimated you'd had a string of lovers before me?"

"I'm not that person anymore."

"Of course you are, Gabriella. People never really change, not deep down inside where it matters. They just pretend to."

"When did you become so cynical, Max?" she asked him sadly. "Did I do that to you?"

"You?" he echoed cuttingly. "Don't flatter yourself!"

The pain inside was growing, roaring through her like a fire feeding on itself until there was nothing left but ashes. For all that she'd promised herself she wouldn't break down in front of him, the scalding pressure behind her eyes signaled how close the tears were, and to her horror she felt her bottom lip quiver uncontrollably.

He noticed. "Don't you dare!" he warned her, in a low, tense voice, starting up from his chair so violently that its metal legs screeched over the pebbled concrete of the terrace. "Don't you *dare* start with the waterworks just because I didn't give you the answers you came looking for! I know that, in the old days, tears always worked for you, but they aren't going to get you what you want this time, at least not from me, so save them for some other fool."

When she first started modeling, there'd been times that she'd found it near impossible to smile for the camera. Days when she'd missed Max so badly, it was all she could do to get out of bed and face another minute without him. Nights when she hadn't been able to sleep for wanting him, and mornings when she'd used so much concealer to hide the shadows under her eyes that her face had felt as if it were encased in mud.

But she'd learned a lot more in the last eighteen months than how to look good on command. She'd learned discipline, and become expert at closing off her emotions behind the remote elegance which had become her trademark.

She called on that discipline now and it did not fail her. The familiar mask slipped into place, not without effort, she had to admit, but well enough that she was able to keep her dignity intact.

"Sorry to disappoint you," she said, rising to her feet with fluid, practiced grace, "but I stopped crying over you so long ago that I've quite forgotten how."

"Don't hand me that. I know what I saw."

She executed a smooth half turn and tossed her parting remark over one provocatively tilted shoulder. "What you saw was a flicker of regret for the mistakes I've made in the past—a passing weakness only because weeping does terrible things to the complexion, especially when one's face is one's fortune. Good night, Max. I've worked hard enough for one day, so if you're feeling energetic, you might try loading our plates and cutlery into the dishwasher—always assuming, of course, that you remember how to open it. Oh, and one more thing. Please don't disturb me when you decide to turn in. I really do need to catch up on my beauty sleep."

# CHAPTER THREE

IF THERE'D been any plausible alternative, he'd have spent the night anywhere but in the same room with her. Since he didn't have that option, he gave her a good two hours' head start before he went up to join her.

She was asleep—or pretending to be—perched so close to the far edge of the mattress, all it would have taken was a gust of air from the open window to topple her to the floor. Being scrupulously careful to leave enough space between them to accommodate a third body, he inched carefully between the sheets on his side of the bed.

Her breathing was light and regular, which made him think perhaps she really was out cold, and eventually he must have dozed off as well because the next thing he knew, it was four in the morning and somehow, while they slept, they'd gravitated toward each other. She lay spooned against him, with her back pressed to his front.

She was wearing a soft cotton nightshirt and it was either very short to begin with, or it had ridden a long way up from where it was supposed to be. He knew because his hand had found its way over her hip so that his fingers were splayed across the bare skin of her warm, taut little belly. A few inches higher and it would have been her breast he was fondling, a realization which put his nether regions onto instant and standing alert.

She stirred. Stretched a little, like a lean, pedigreed cat. Rolled over until she was half facing him. In the opaque light of predawn, he saw her eyes drift open. Then, as awareness chased away sleep, she grew very still and very, very wary.

For about half a second, they stared at one another, then simultaneously rolled away from each other. She retreated to her side of the bed again and he slunk off to the bathroom, telling himself his problem was that he had to pee.

It hadn't been the problem then, and it wasn't the problem three hours later when he found himself suffering the same physical reaction all over again at the sight of his wife—his *estranged* wife! he reminded himself for about the fiftieth time—presiding over the breakfast table and looking even more delicious than the food on his plate.

"Are you coming with me to the airport this afternoon?" she asked him, her tone suggesting she'd be hard-pressed to notice whether he did or not.

Regarding her over the top of the morning paper, Max had found himself wondering if there was something in the bottled drinking water she favored which allowed her to remain so cool and aloof, when it was all he could do not to break out in a sweat at the thought of the night just past.

"I wasn't planning on it," he said, trying to match her nonchalance. "It's been a while since your parents last saw you. I imagine they'd like to have you to themselves for a while."

*Nonchalant?* What a laugh! He sounded as stilted as a rank amateur trying out for a spot on some third-rate TV commercial! Not that she noticed. She simply gave that impassive little shrug of hers, waved the coffeepot under his nose, and said, "May I give you refill?"

He didn't know what time she'd slipped out of bed, but it must have been early. Not only had she ground fresh coffee beans and made fresh fruit syrup for his waffles, she'd also found time to repair her manicure. Her nails gleamed pale rose against the brushed steel of the carafe.

As for the rest of her...oh, brother! Sleek and elegant in a floor-length, blue-and-purple patterned thing which was neither bathrobe nor dress but something in between; with not a hair out of place and looking as fresh as the morning dew, she gave new meaning to the term "picture perfect."

"No," he said, slapping down the paper and shoving back from the table. "I have to get going." *Quickly, before his imagination ran riot feeding itself on memories of the night before and he made a further fool of himself!*

"When do you expect to be back?"

"As late as possible. That way, there'll be less risk of us screwing up the charade."

Her eyes, pure turquoise in the morning light, pinned him in an unwavering stare. "But you *will* join us for dinner?"

"Of course. That's part of our arrangement."

"And you will remember it's going to take more than just your putting in an appearance to carry all this off?"

"How much more?" he asked, more to annoy her than because he cared about her answer.

"As much as it takes," she said.

The remark stayed with him all day, a major but not, he was surprised to discover, unpleasant distraction. By the time he let himself into the penthouse late that afternoon, his dread at what the next two weeks might bring had been diluted by a peculiar anticipation. Damned if he understood why, but having Gabriella underfoot again charged his energy like nothing else had in months!

Stopping by his office to drop off his briefcase, he stood a moment at the partially open sliding doors, unnoticed by the threesome seated a few yards away at the table on the roof garden. He didn't need to understand the language to recognize a certain tension in the conversation taking place between his wife and his in-laws.

Still strikingly handsome despite failing health, Zoltan sat ramrod-straight in one of the cushioned chairs, his dark eyes watchful as Gabriella replied to something her mother had said. Maria Siklossy, a little heavier than she'd been two years ago, leaned forward, consternation written all over her face.

Gabriella, polished and perfect as ever in a dress which he'd have called washed-out green but which probably deserved a fancier description, traced her finger over the condensation beading her glass. From her stream of fluent Hungarian, only three words had meaning for Max: Tokyo, Rome, and Vancouver.

He didn't have to be a rocket scientist to figure she was trying to justify keeping three addresses while her husband made do with one, and that neither Zoltan nor Maria was buying any of it. Loosening his tie and rolling back the cuffs of his shirt, Max waded in to do his bit toward easing the old couple's concerns.

If the relief that washed over Gabriella's face when she saw him was any indication, he'd timed his entrance perfectly. Springing up from her chair like a greyhound let loose on the racetrack, she exclaimed, "You're home, Max! I didn't expect you until later."

"Missed you too much to stay away any longer, baby cakes," he said, immersing himself in his appointed role with gleeful relish.

Her mouth fell open. *"Baby cakes?"*

The opportunity was too good to pass up. Sweeping her into his arms, he planted a lengthy kiss on those deliciously parted lips. She smelled of wood violets and tasted of wild cherries.

Her eyes, wide open and startled, stared into his. Briefly, she resisted his embrace, then sort of collapsed against him. Her small firm breasts pressed against his chest. Their tips grew hard. Her cheeks flushed pink.

Fleetingly, he considered wallowing in the moment, if only to enjoy her disconcertion. Why not? He hadn't asked to be cast as the romantic hero in her little production, but since it had been thrust upon him anyway, he might as well get his kicks wherever he happened to find them.

At least, that's how he tried rationalizing his actions. But, just like the night before and the morning after, another part of his anatomy had different ideas and showed itself ready to play its part with animated enthusiasm. So, reluctantly, before she realized the state she'd reduced him to, he backed off slightly but kept her anchored next to him as he turned to greet her parents.

"Good to see you again, Zoltan," he said, shaking his father-in-law's hand. "You, too, Maria. Welcome to Canada."

He bent to kiss her cheek, peripherally aware of the tears in her eyes as she held his face between her palms and murmured approving little Hungarian noises, but most of his attention remained focused on Gabriella. Her waist, half spanned by his hand, felt shockingly frail. Though he didn't test the theory there and then, he was pretty sure he could have counted every rib through her clothes.

Pasting on his most affable expression to disguise his concern, he said, "So, what's everyone drinking?"

"Iced tea," Gabriella murmured faintly. "Would you like some?"

He smiled into her eyes which had a sort of glazed look to them. "We can celebrate your parents' arrival with something more exciting than that, surely? How about champagne—unless you'd prefer something stronger, Zoltan?''

''A glass of wine would be pleasant.''

He might have temporarily quieted Maria's suspicions, but he had a long way to go with the old man, Max realized. Zoltan was watching him like a hawk about to dine on a very fat mouse.

''Fine. I'll go do the honors.'' Suddenly feeling about as uncomfortable as he had the night he'd been discovered almost stark naked in the Siklossy palace, Max took off around the southeast corner of the terrace to the kitchen entrance, and left Gabriella to clear the iced tea paraphernalia off the table.

She followed soon after and plunked the tray of glasses on the kitchen counter with a clatter. ''What was *that* all about?'' she demanded, her color still high.

''Being a good host,'' he said, knowing damn well she wasn't referring to his suggesting champagne, but deciding to play dumb anyway. ''What are you serving for dinner?''

''Broiled salmon. But another stunt like the one you just pulled, and you might find yourself being the one shoved in the oven!''

''Your English gets better all the time, Gabriella,'' he remarked, hauling a nineteen ninety-seven Pol Roger out of the refrigerator and inspecting the label. ''Very idiomatic indeed. I'm impressed.''

''Well, I'm not! Who did you think you were fooling just now with that ridiculous exhibition?''

''Your mother, certainly. And if your father still has any doubts about us, I'll make short work of them, as well.''

''Not with a repeat performance like the one you just put on, I assure you.''

"Are you saying you didn't enjoy our little exchange?"

"Certainly not!" But she blushed an even deeper shade of pink.

"Keep telling fibs like this, Gabriella," he informed her genially, "and your nose will grow so long, you'll never model again. Come on, admit it. You practically fainted with pleasure when I kissed you."

"That wasn't pleasure, it was shock."

"Shock?" He rotated the bottle of champagne until the cork slipped out with a subdued and well-bred pop. "I fail to see why. Weren't you the one who lectured me just this morning on the need to act the part of besotted husband?"

"*Devoted*, Max, not besotted, and certainly not... *lecherous!* The next time you feel disposed to show your affection, don't get so carried away." She piled goose liver pâté and crackers on a square slab of glass which he now realized was some sort of serving dish but which he'd been using as a doorstop, dressed the whole works up with bits of parsley, and arranged a fan of cocktail napkins on the side. "And don't ever call me 'baby cakes' again! I've never heard anything so ridiculous in my life."

Scowling, he watched her march off. Blast the woman, anyway! She was as contrary as hell, and damned if he could read her mood from one minute to the next. Just when he thought he had a fix on her, she did an about-face that made him wonder if he'd ever scratch below her surface and find out what was really going on in her head.

Dinner was a never-ending nightmare, a minefield of disaster waiting to explode. Questions which would have been a breeze to answer if a person had nothing to hide required the most delicate handling, and the effort to appear happy and at ease taxed Gabriella to the limit.

As for Max—oh, she'd have cheerfully throttled *him*, if it weren't that he wasn't worth serving time in jail for! Smiling, urbane, doing and saying all the right things, without a single false step. Treating her mother as if she were a queen, deferring to her father in the choice of wines with the meal. And all the time sending her, his wife, glances brimming with mischief. Putting on a show that went above and beyond anything she'd had in mind when she'd persuaded him to take part in an undertaking which was turning out to be much more complicated than even she'd bargained for.

Her parents might have been charmed at the way he held out her chair at the dining table then, when she was least expecting it, leaned over and kissed the side of her neck, but she'd been so flustered she'd almost knocked the silver sauceboat of Béarnaise into her father's lap!

By the time she'd brought herself under control again, he was up to further mischief, flirting disgracefully with her mother. "Maria, I'm hurt you'd even ask!" he practically crooned, his sexy, Canadian baritone sliding the length of the table to wrap itself around Gabriella's senses like rich velvet. "Of course I'll be booking time off from work to take you sight-seeing. In fact, it occurred to me you might even like to travel a bit farther afield, once you're over your jet lag. What do you think, Gabriella? Shall we take them to Banff and show them the Rockies? I could charter a private jet to avoid the lengthy drive."

*"What do I think?"* she hissed, the minute she got him alone in the kitchen between courses. "I think you've lost your mind, that's what! Who are you trying to impress with all your talk of chartering a jet?"

"Why, who else but your parents, dear heart," he said

equably, attempting to feign injured innocence and succeeding only in looking as crafty as a wolf on the prowl. "I'm just trying to be helpful and live up to my end of our bargain."

"Stop trying so hard," she fairly spat.

He put down the second bottle of wine he'd just taken from the refrigerator and made for the swing door connecting to the dining room. "Okay. I'll go tell them I've had second thoughts and Banff in July isn't such a good idea. Too many flowers, too much sunshine—and too much you."

"You'll do no such thing, Max Logan!"

He paused with one hand poised to push open the door. "Hell, Gabriella, make up your mind. Do you want my help in getting through the next two weeks and sending your folks home happy, or not?"

"I want your help," she said feebly. The trouble was, she wanted a whole lot more than that, and being near him again—having him so close that she could smell his aftershave and the special scent of his skin and his hair, and the soap he used in the shower…oh, they filled her senses so thoroughly, she could barely think straight.

She wasn't completely stupid, though. She'd seen the way he'd sidled out of bed when he'd found her cuddled up next to him during the night. Heavens, he hadn't been able to get away from her fast enough! And when he'd returned, the way he'd hunched his back toward her and yanked the sheet up around his shoulders had told her plainly enough that he could hardly wait to have the bed to himself again. How would they ever keep up appearances if they were flung together all day while they acted as tour guides for her parents?

"But don't you find it hard on your marriage, with your wife away so much of the time?" her father was asking, when Gabriella finally pulled herself together enough to return to the dining room with the apricot torte dessert.

It was precisely the kind of question she dreaded, and almost enough to make her flee to the kitchen again.

Max, however, didn't turn a hair. "Gabriella wanted to pursue a career. I didn't see it as my right to interfere with that."

"But you're her husband!" Her father gave the table a gentle but emphatic thump that set the ice in the water goblets to chiming like little bells.

"Her husband, yes, but not her keeper, Zoltan."

"It would not do for me. In my day, being a wife was all the career a woman could want."

Feeling obliged to contribute something to the discussion, Gabriella set the torte on the table and, resting her hand on Max's shoulder in a splendid display of marital unity, said, "Times have changed, Father. And things are different in North America."

"Different, perhaps, but not, I think, better. You belong exactly where you stand right now—at your husband's side."

"It's a long commute from Rome or Tokyo to Vancouver, Zoltan," Max said lightly. "The camera loves Gabriella, and a certain amount of separation comes with the territory when a man finds himself married to a model as much in demand as my wife's become." He turned a disgracefully angelic look Gabriella's way. "Isn't that right, my love?"

"Yes," she murmured. "Absolutely."

"And then there's her age to think about," he went on. "She's not getting any younger and this is definitely a young woman's game. She might as well make the most of it before her looks start to go."

Oh, the rogue! It was all she could do not to push his

face into his dessert! ''I'm only just twenty-four, for heaven's sake!''

''Is that what you're telling people these days?'' He smiled at her benignly, before switching his attention back to her father. ''Ah well, even you must agree that it's the quality of time spent together that counts, Zoltan.''

''Those terrible newspapers say you live apart because you cannot live together,'' her mother put in, finally giving voice to the one area of her marriage Gabriella most dreaded having to explain.

As if he felt the tremor that passed over her, Max covered Gabriella's hand with his and gave it a squeeze. ''Which is precisely why they're terrible, Maria. They thrive on sensationalism, not truth.''

''Even so, how can there be babies, if...?''

''I'm sure Gabriella will have babies,'' he said smoothly. ''In time.''

What he didn't say was that, if she did, they wouldn't be his. He'd made it abundantly clear he wasn't interested in fathering children with her. ''I'd throw a party, except there's nothing in any of this to celebrate,'' he'd said bitterly, when she confessed she'd been mistaken about the pregnancy. ''Kids deserve parents committed to something a bit more compelling than the fact that one felt obligated to marry the other. There won't be any more such *mistakes,* Gabriella.''

He'd made sure that there weren't. Whenever he came to her bed after that, he brought a condom with him.

''Don't wait too long,'' her mother said wistfully. ''Zoltan and I are no longer young, and I would so love to hold a grandchild in my arms before I die.''

Gabriella knew that the quaver in her mother's voice and the pain in her eyes meant she was remembering the son who'd died during the revolution, and it was all she could do not to cry out, *I'll give you a grandchild, Mama, I will! A little boy called Stefan, just like my brother!*

But there was a limit to how far she'd take the duplicity. Being near him again left her convinced there'd never be any other man for her but Max, and she would not make promises she knew she couldn't keep.

"I don't know that I can do this after all," she told him, once her parents, worn out from the long journey, had made an early night of it. "Two weeks of pretending, of telling lies... Max, it's turning out to be so much harder than I thought it would be, and we still have thirteen days to go!"

They were in the kitchen again, and she was putting away the last of the dishes they'd used at dinner. The kitchen seemed to be the place they always did the most talking, perhaps because it was the least intimate room in the penthouse and so the one least likely to stir up pointless longings.

Not that Max suffered from any of *them,* as his next comment proved. "Time was that lying came so easily to you, you never gave it a second thought," he said, standing in the open doorway to the terrace and looking out at the brightly lit city skyline. "Guess you're a bit out of practice, my dear."

For a moment, she stared at him. At the white dress shirt lying smoothly across his big shoulders, at the sun-dark nape of his neck and his thick, black hair, and the long elegant line of his spine.

Just so had she first come across him: from behind, in the garden at her parents' home in Budapest. She'd known before he turned around and she saw his face that he'd be more beautiful than any man she'd ever met. Had recognized, within five minutes of looking into his blue, blue eyes, that she was in love with him and would remain so for the rest of her life.

Silly, girlish notions that had no bearing on the way things were today! Swallowing the tears which seemed never to be far from the surface where he was concerned, she said bitterly, ''Perhaps because I no longer need to lie in order to find acceptance from the people around me.''

He spared her a brief, backward glance. ''Has it been worth it, Gabriella—all the fame and fortune you've won? Have they been worth the price you've paid for them?''

''What price? I had nothing to lose to begin with.''

''You had a husband and a marriage, things you once claimed you wanted more than anything else on earth.''

''Those I still have.''

''In name only.''

She dried the last of the hand-washed wineglasses— slender, lovely things, delicately crafted. ''That was your choice, Max. I was prepared to stay and try to make our marriage work.''

His laugh told her what he thought of that reply. ''You were gone within six months. I'd hardly call that hanging in over the long haul!''

''And you did nothing to stop me.''

''Would you have stayed, if I'd tried?''

''No,'' she said, fighting to keep her voice steady because, by then, she was losing the battle with the tears which blurred her vision and turned the wineglass she still held into an iridescent bubble. ''Because you didn't want me. You've never wanted me.''

He'd always hated it when she cried and more than once had accused her of turning on the waterworks as a means of getting her own way. If he realized she was crying now, he'd say something cruel like, *Save the tears for someone who cares.* Or worse, *No, I never did. Isn't it nice that we at last agree on something?*

Determined not to give him the satisfaction, she swiped at her eyes with a corner of the tea towel and, in doing so, knocked the wineglass out of her hand. It hit the granite counter with a brutal crash.

*"Oh!"*

The sound of splintering crystal, almost musical compared to her wail of dismay, brought Max spinning around to see what had happened. Bending her head to hide her misery, she began scooping the fragments into a tidy heap and found that the stem of the glass, still intact, had snapped cleanly off the bowl. Such a pity!

"Watch what you're doing!" He crossed the kitchen floor in rapid strides and pulled her hands away from the debris. "For Pete's sake, Gabriella, you're dripping blood all over everything."

Amazed, she stared at the thin line of scarlet beads forming along the side of her finger. How was it possible that she'd sustained such a wound, yet felt no pain? And if one part of her could remain numb to injury, why couldn't another? Why did the raging ache in her heart keep getting worse?

Unable to face the answer, she took what was left of the bowl of the glass and tried placing it on top of the severed stem. "Perhaps if I keep all the pieces, it can be put back together again. I know they do marvelous things these days to repair broken treasures."

For all that she tried to control herself, her words came out on a sob and the infernal tears broke loose and rolled off the end of her nose. Oh, what a mess she must look, and how repelled he must be at the sight of her!

Oddly, though, his voice was full of something other than the contempt she expected. It was warm and rather kind. "I'm afraid it'd take a miracle, honey. This thing's past repair. Let's just sweep the whole mess into the garbage can and forget it."

"But it's one of twelve we received as a wedding gift, Max," she whimpered. "Now the set's incomplete."

"Well, that's a shame, but you ought to know by now there are some things that can't be mended, no matter how much you wish they could be."

"Sort of like us, when you think about it," she said wistfully. "We're supposed to be a couple, but we're not. There's no bond to hold us together."

*Dear heaven, where was her pride? She sounded as plaintive as a tragedy queen about to breathe her last!*

Of course, he noticed. "Let's not turn a minor accident into a melodrama!" he said, hurriedly putting the safety of the kitchen counter between them as if he feared she might fling herself at his feet and beg him to toss her a crumb of affection.

If nothing else, his unsympathetic about-face snapped her out of the well of self-pity she'd been about to drown in. She grabbed a tissue from the box on the shelf next to the telephone desk, folded it around her finger in a makeshift bandage, then took another and used it to sweep the shards of glass into the waste bin. "You're absolutely right, for once. Some things are broken beyond repair."

*Including our marriage, and the sooner I face up to that, the better off I'll be!*

He was watching her, his expression inscrutable. "If it were my business to begin with, I'd tell you you look like hell. You sure you're feeling okay?"

It took some effort, but she managed to brush off his concern with an airy, "Now who's making something out of nothing?"

"I'm not talking about your finger," he said, coming

back to where she stood and tilting up her chin so that she had no choice but to return his steady gaze. "It's the rest of you that has me wondering. Do you get enough rest?"

"Since you mention it, as a rule, yes. But the last few weeks, and the last couple of days in particular, have been stressful. Contrary to what you might choose to think, I don't enjoy deceiving my parents."

"Then why not tell them the truth and have done with it?"

"Oh, Max, you already know why!" She sighed and massaged her temples wearily. "You can't have missed how much they've aged in the last two years, especially my father. Divorce goes against everything he and my mother believe in, and it would kill him to learn our marriage is a failure. It would be different if they lived on our doorstep and could see for themselves that life goes on even when a couple breaks up, but they're half a world away geographically, and belong to a different era. They don't understand the modern way of doing things and I don't have it in me to destroy their illusions. What's the harm in letting them think our marriage is strong like theirs?"

"Plenty, if it has you tied up in knots like this."

"It's just a headache. I get them sometimes when I'm under pressure."

Turning her around, he began kneading the tense muscles in her shoulders. The warmth of his touch, the strength of his fingers probing her flesh to seek out and relieve each sore spot, left her sagging. She leaned both hands on the counter. Her neck drooped, unable to support the weight of her head. Her legs turned to jelly.

She was wearing a low-backed dress held up by a halter strap. He pressed his thumbs lightly over each exposed vertebra. His breath a caress at her ear, he asked, "Is this helping?"

His magician's touch was draining her, leaving her weak as a kitten. She could barely summon the energy to say, "More than you can…begin to imagine."

Methodically, his thumbs traveled lower. She heard the subdued purr of her zipper opening. Felt his palms radiating from her spine to encompass her ribs in soothing, ever-widening circles, until his fingertips almost brushed the sides of her breasts.

*Soothing?* Oh, who was she deceiving this time? Electrifying was what it was. Thrilling. The most sensuous, drugging delight she'd ever known!

She felt his breath in her hair and then, astoundingly, his lips, warm and damp, at her ear. His kiss, soft as a snowflake, deadly as an earthquake, thundered to the inner depths of her soul.

What began as a moan of pure pleasure evolved into a drawn-out murmuring of his name. "M…a…xxx…!"

She should have kept her mouth shut. The sound of her voice jarring the outer silence broke whatever spell he'd been weaving. The kiss ended. Abruptly, he removed his hands, drew up her zipper and stepped away. "Ten minutes in the hot tub would do you more good than this," he said harshly.

Of course, she knew ahead of time that the question was pointless, but she asked it anyway. "Will you join me?"

Already halfway to the front hall, he flung his reply over his shoulder. "No, thanks. I brought work home and should get to it. Hope you sleep better tonight."

How *dare* he offer her a glimpse of paradise, then, when she was almost fainting with longing, snatch it away again? Waspish with disappointment, she snapped,

"There'll be a better chance of that if you wear pajamas to bed."

*That* stopped his flying exit! "How do you know I didn't last night?" he said.

"Your torso wasn't covered when I woke up this morning—not by the bed linen, and not by anything else."

"Why, shame on you, Gabriella!" he chided. "Were you spying on me while I slept?"

"Spying, my left foot! I'm not blind, Max, and a man your size is pretty hard to miss."

She should have been more specific and said *A man with shoulders the size of yours is hard to miss,* because he turned to her, a grin inching over his face, and she knew exactly what he was referring to when he said, "I'm going to take that as a compliment, my dear."

She refused to blush and she refused to look away. Instead, determined to have the last word for a change *and* pay him back for his earlier remark about her age, she said, "You'd be a lot better off going on a diet. I can't say I paid too much attention, but it looked to me as if you're running to fat."

Considering she had yet to set eyes on a more gorgeously put-together specimen than Max Logan—in *every* respect!—her parting shot was nothing less than a bald-faced lie. And the way his laughter followed her as she fled past him and scuttled up the stairs told her he knew it as well as she did.

Once inside the bedroom, she collapsed into a chair, her heart pitter-pattering like an overwound toy. With care and a lot of luck, she might make it safely through the next thirteen days. But the nights?

Dear Lord, the nights were a different matter altogether!

## CHAPTER FOUR

THE next several days passed uneventfully enough. She took her parents sight-seeing and shopping, and was glad when they confessed they'd find traveling further afield too exhausting. In truth, she preferred a less-hectic pace herself and was content to spend quiet hours alone with them.

It was a happy, serene time, full of sunlight and laughter. And most of all, of love. It flowed over and around Gabriella from every quarter—except for the space occasionally occupied by her husband. His little corner exuded pure, malevolent mischief!

Then, on the Thursday, he phoned just as she was cleaning up the kitchen after serving her parents a late breakfast. "Check the society column in today's newspaper," he said shortly, obviously so put out by whatever it contained that he felt disinclined to preface the order with anything as civil as "Good morning." "Your arrival in town hasn't gone unnoticed. Better be prepared for the rest of the media to horn in on the fact. My assistant's already fielding calls at the office."

"Interviews go with the territory in my profession," Gabriella replied breezily. "I've grown quite accustomed to handling them."

"No doubt. But how comfortable are you going to be if someone shoves a microphone in your face and asks if there's any truth to the rumors that our marriage is in trouble? From the way you coped the other night when your mother aired the same question, it's my guess you'll have a tough time coming up with any sort of convincing answer. Where are your mom and dad, by the way? Not listening in, I hope?''

''No, Max,'' she informed him, matching his sarcasm and then some. ''It would never occur to them to eavesdrop on a private conversation. They're far too well bred. If you must know, my father's in the pool, and my mother's being a good wife and watching to make sure he doesn't overdo it. As for your other concern, should a reporter approach me and want details of my relationship with you, I'll say what I always say—that my private life isn't open for discussion.''

''Dear heart,'' he sneered, ''it's already under the public microscope. You show up after months away and there's no loving husband at the airport to meet your flight. Instead, you're caught on camera looking as grim as if you've just been handed a life sentence behind bars. Then you're seen hitting all the high spots around town in the company of two elderly guests, but still no sign of the errant husband in tow. Face it, Gabriella, the situation calls for a little damage control.''

She recognized from the take-charge tone in his voice that he already had a plan in mind. ''And how do you propose we go about it?''

''Lunch,'' he said. ''You, me, and the parents, at my club. This morning's columnist's always hanging around the place looking for gossip, so we might as well hand him his daily quota up front and save him the trouble of having to do any more speculating. I'll send a car to collect you at eleven-thirty.''

The car, as she might have expected, was not a plain taxi as she'd been using, but a long, black limousine with a uniformed driver at the wheel. Except for his raised eyebrows, which might have indicated approval or criti-

cism of such extravagance, her father made no comment.
Her mother, though, was charmed.

"So lovely," she breathed, sinking into the luxurious
leather upholstery, her air of appreciation for fine things
harking back to happier days when being a member of
the Hungarian aristocracy had gone hand in hand with
wealth. "Elegant and dignified, the way life used to be
for us, before."

She didn't need to elaborate. Gabriella had heard that
same qualification from the time she'd been born.
Everything about today was compared to the way things
had been *before the troubles*. Some people had adjusted
to the changes they brought; her parents, especially her
mother, had not. They had lost too much, including a son.

Max was waiting outside when the car drew up under
the canopied entrance to his club. Before the driver had
a chance to do the honors, he opened the door and taking
Gabriella by the hand, ushered her out. Not about to be
thrown into confusion by another of his phony displays
of affection, she gave him a hurried peck on the cheek,
then immediately stepped a safe distance away before in-
quiring, "Have we kept you waiting long?"

"Not at all, my love." It was another sunny day and
he was wearing dark glasses, so she couldn't see the expression in his eyes, but the thread of amusement in his
voice and that ironic endearment told her he'd noticed
how she'd fairly bolted away from him. "I got here only
a couple of minutes ago myself."

He'd reserved a table overlooking the harbor and preor-
dered from the club's excellent wine cellar. But neither
the vintage Pinot Gris nor the cold prawns vinaigrette
quite managed to dim Gabriella's awareness of his knee
pressed too close to hers under the table, or the way he'd
ever so casually manage to nudge her shoulder or brush

his fingers against hers under one pretext after another. *Pass me the rolls, will you, Gabriella? Here, my love, have a little more dressing. What do you think, sweetheart, shall we order strawberries for dessert?*

It was all for show, she knew, and she supposed she ought to be grateful that he was working so hard to maintain the myth of husbandly devotion. But his proximity, close enough that she could feel his heat, see the new beard growth already stippling his jaw, and inhale the scent of his aftershave, was driving her to distraction.

*Stop touching me!* she wanted to scream. *Stop stealing the air from my lungs and making my heart flop around like a landed fish!*

Of course, she did no such thing. Even if the society columnist seated two tables away hadn't been mentally photographing every nuance and gesture so avidly that it was a wonder he didn't fall off his chair, her parents' unalloyed relief at such an exhibition of marital bliss made it worth what it cost her to suffer in silence. Only later, after Max had insisted on taking the afternoon off to spend a little more time with them, did she realize she hadn't begun to pay nearly dearly enough.

They'd come out of the art gallery and were headed back to where the limousine waited when her mother paused to admire a display of diamond rings in the shop window of a well-known jeweler. "Such lovely things," she sighed, "but not, I think, as beautiful as your wedding band which I notice you are not wearing, Gabriella."

At a loss—for how could she say, *I left it behind when I walked away from my marriage and don't know what my husband did with it?*—Gabriella turned helplessly to Max. "When Gabriella's traveling, we keep it in the safe at home," he said. "That way, there's less chance of it being lost or stolen."

"But she is not traveling now," her father said pointedly. "And it seems to me that a wife should always wear the symbol of her marriage, especially when she is away from her husband, as a reminder of what is most important in her life."

As if the mere idea that Gabriella could easily forget him was too funny for words, Max laughed and pressed a bell set discreetly beside the outer door of the shop. "Since you're taken with the things in the window, Maria, come inside and meet the man who created them. Gio Salvatore's an old acquaintance of mine and I'm sure he'll be delighted to show you other examples of his work."

The atmosphere inside the shop, so hushed it was almost reverent, reminded Gabriella of a church. The sleek glass display cases, lined with opulent black velvet and made all the more dramatic with artfully concealed spotlights, provided a perfect setting for the finely crafted work on show.

Like the decor, Gio Salvatore himself was a man of tasteful restraint. Immaculately turned out in a navy three-piece suit, his platinum-silver hair rivaling that of some of his creations, he emerged from a back room when informed of his visitors, and greeted Max with obvious pleasure.

"I'm honored," he said, gesturing expansively to Gabriella and her parents after the introductions were made. "Please, if there's a piece you would like to examine more closely, you have only to ask."

Max, all benign smiles and easy authority, saw her mother's reluctance and urged her closer to the showcases. "Don't be shy, Maria. If something takes your fancy, try it on."

"No," she said. "I would like to look, that's all."

But her gaze lingered on the lovely pieces and Gabriella

knew she was remembering the things they'd been forced to sell in order to effect basic repairs to their home and country estate. "The reason," her father had explained, when Gabriella at ten had asked why her mama never wore the diamond necklace and pendant earrings shown in the portrait of her hanging over the mantel in the main salon, "is that they are luxuries we can no longer afford. Although we are members of the old aristocracy and the property we lost for so long has finally been returned to us, we are, like many of our friends, penniless."

Since she'd found success, Gabriella had tried many times to make their lives easier, but her parents had steadfastly refused to let her give them money. It had taken all her considerable powers of persuasion to make them accept the gift of airline tickets so that they could visit her in Canada—and only then, she suspected, because they believed their traveling years were coming to an end and they couldn't bear to pass up the chance to see how she lived in her adopted country.

"Mama," she whispered now, "it would make me very happy if you would please choose something and let me buy it for you as a souvenir of your visit."

"What do such fine things matter?" her mother replied, stroking her hand. "To know that you and Max are so much in love is worth more to me than all the jewels in the world."

Had old age left the mother more susceptible to being hoodwinked, or was it that the daughter had become so adept at deceit that she could fool even her own parent? The question shamed Gabriella and left her eyes so hot with unshed tears that she had to turn away.

Like a watchful bodyguard, Max materialized at her side. "Sweetheart," he said with uncommon gentleness, bracing her with an arm around her shoulders and forcibly removing her from her mother's shrewd observation, "there's a piece over here that you have to see. If it weren't that the gold work is a little too much for a neck as slender as yours, it might almost have been made especially for you."

Shielding her with his body, he steered her to the other side of the shop and pointed out an emerald-cut aquamarine pendant set in a gold filigree chain studded with small but exquisite diamonds.

He meant to be kind; to divert attention away from her distress and give her the chance to recover herself. But tenderness and compassion were not his habit with her and she was in too fragile a state to accept them with equanimity. The aquamarine flared with light, its edges fractured into prisms of brilliant fire by the tears seeping from her eyes.

"This won't do," he murmured, producing a handkerchief and passing it to her. "You're going to give the game away if you keep on like this."

"My mother thinks we're in love, Max!" she snuffled. "How can I let her remain in ignorance?"

"Perhaps you can't. Perhaps this is too great a deception, even for you. But before you decide to lay out the truth, consider what hearing it will cost her. Are you really prepared to make her pay that high a price, Gabriella?"

She drew in a shuddering breath. "No. Whether that might have been the right thing to do at the beginning is beside the point. We've set out along this path, and it's too late to turn back now. I just didn't know I'd find it so...so...."

*Painful being near you. Knowing we're going through the motions only when what I most wish is that the feelings between us were real instead of make-believe.*

"Difficult?" he suggested, noticing her hesitation.

"My goodness, Gabriella, can it be that your high-profile success has forced you to develop a conscience? Or is all this breast-beating just another attempt to make a fool of me?"

Thanks to his thoughtfulness, she'd almost managed to bring her emotions under control, but the sudden about-face to his usual self unraveled her so thoroughly that she wanted to slap him. Hard!

She refrained, not because it would have laid bare their mockery of a marriage but because, regardless of whatever mistakes she'd made in the past, she *was* a Siklossy by blood, and she refused to let him reduce her to behaving like a savage. "Oh!" she muttered instead, flexing her fingers convulsively. "Just when I begin to find myself almost liking the man I married, you remind me what a wasted effort it is!"

Surprisingly, he didn't come back with an equally searing reply. If anything, he looked almost subdued. "I guess I asked for that," he said quietly. "My remark was uncalled for and I apologize. It looks as if we're both finding this more of a strain than we bargained for. Why don't I go keep your parents entertained while you compose yourself? When you feel ready to face them, I'll phone for the car to pick you up here and take you home."

"You're not coming with us?"

*Don't be foolish, Gabriella! It's better that he doesn't.*

"No." He glanced at his watch. "I need to get back to the office. And before I forget, I won't be home for dinner tonight."

"Oh, Max, why not? I was counting on you to be there!"

"Because," he informed her severely, "to accommodate you, I canceled a previous lunch engagement and have had to reschedule it for this evening."

Unreasonably disappointed, she said, "Oh, really? And I suppose the next thing you're going to tell me is that it's business?"

He stared at her and waited a heartbeat before replying coldly, "It's certainly not *your* business, Gabriella."

Something about the way he turned aside her question reminded her of her first night back at the penthouse...

*Have you been with another woman, Max? I want to know the truth.*

*I doubt you could handle it in this instance...*

"Why not?" she flared with sudden disquieting fury. "Because you're meeting the woman you as good as admitted you've been seeing while I was away?"

She could no more miss the grimace of distaste that crossed his face at her outburst, than she could suppress the demons of jealousy which she'd allowed to goad her into asking such a question in the first place. "Well, naturally!" he said, his voice and eyes chilly as a midwinter's day. "Our assignations always take place in my office. I usually have my wicked way with her on my desk once everyone else has vacated the premises. Of course, we have to be careful we don't get caught by the night cleaning staff, but that just adds a bit of extra spice to the whole business. Is that what you wanted to hear?"

"No," she said, so mortified she couldn't look at him. "Go to her with my blessing. Stay out all night, if you wish."

He'd be doing her a favor if he did! She'd already come too close to having him break her heart all over again, and they'd been together only a few days. The more reason he gave her to mistrust and despise him, the easier it would be, at the end of their two weeks, to say goodbye to him and walk away whole.

"I doubt I'll go quite that far," he said, barely managing to smother a grin, "but it could be late when I get back so don't wait up for me."

"I wouldn't dream of it. And please don't let me delay you any further. Thank you for a very nice lunch. I hope your…dinner is everything you'd like it to be."

"You're welcome, and thank you. I expect it will."

Rather than endure another farcical display of affection, she turned away from him and, pretending an interest in a sapphire-and-platinum starburst brooch pinned behind the glass of a wall display, glared miserably at his reflection as he stopped to say a few words to her parents, then strode to the door.

Like Gio Salvatore, he wore a beautifully tailored suit, but where the jeweler looked dapper in navy, her husband exuded raw power in charcoal-gray. He was cut out for the ruthless world of business, not domestic bliss, and in all fairness, he'd never led her to believe otherwise.

When she learned that she wasn't pregnant, he hadn't for a moment pretended regret. That he'd even proposed to her in the first place was because he was a man of honor, of ethics. He believed in being held accountable for his mistakes, and he did not willingly renege on a deal—not even one as flimsy as their marriage had turned out to be. How else to explain that he'd done nothing to end it?

*That,* she acknowledged sadly, would be up to her, and the sooner she went about it, the better, after all. Because leaving herself open to the kind of sordid, gnawing uncertainty currently plaguing her was too undignified to be countenanced.

Rather than face the evening knowing she'd be listening all the while for his key at the door, she took her parents out for an early dinner to a pretty little French restaurant a few blocks away.

Afterward, they strolled along the seawall and got back to the penthouse just after nine. To Gabriella's surprise, Max was already there, sprawled on the sofa in the living room. He'd exchanged his suit for a pair of blue jeans, and his dress shirt for a sports shirt.

*Because there were lipstick stains on his collar, perhaps?*

His hair wore the rumpled look that comes of having fingers raked through it.

*His own—or his dinner date's?*

"Hey," he said, springing up and offering his seat to her mother, "I was beginning to wonder if I should be organizing a search party. What happened, did the limo driver take the long way 'round when he brought you home?"

The words were uttered lightly, but his smile seemed forced and if the idea hadn't been completely preposterous, Gabriella would have thought he'd been worried by their absence. "We went out for dinner," she said, dropping her bag on a side table. "I didn't feel like cooking."

"Well, try leaving a note the next time, my love. If I'd known where you were, I'd have joined you."

"You said you were dining out and wouldn't be home until much later," she reminded him sweetly.

"I changed my mind." He came to where she stood and stroked his knuckles along her jaw. "Where'd you go?"

*"Pierre's."*

"That's some distance away. How'd you get there and back?"

"We walked," she said. "For heaven's sake, Max, if

I were to quiz you like this, you'd waste no time telling me to mind my own business!''

"It's a husband's prerogative to be concerned when his wife goes missing and she's as well known as you are,'' he said sharply. "The streets aren't as safe at night as they once were, you know.''

*Concerned? Suspicious* was more like it—and a tiny, mean-spirited part of her rejoiced in the fact. What was sauce for the goose, after all, was sauce for the gander, too!

Her tone equally astringent, she said, "I was hardly missing, nor was I alone. And you seem to forget I'm used to taking care of myself.''

As if he realized their exchange had strayed from natural curiosity to barely veiled hostility, Max kissed her lightly on the lips and said, "You're right, and I apologize. You had no way of knowing my plans had changed.''

"As a matter of interest, why did they?''

"The person I'd hoped to meet couldn't make it.''

*The person? How about ''the other woman'', Max?* she thought bitterly, irked at the ease with which he turned the tables on her small victory.

Masking her rancor behind a smile so dripping with saccharine sweetness that she almost gagged, she said, "What a shame! Were you terribly disappointed?''

"Not really. Rather pleased, in fact. You and I spend few enough evenings together as it is, and I was particularly looking forward to tonight because I have something for you.''

He left the room and she heard him cross the hall and enter his study. Shortly after, he returned with a bottle of cognac and two leather jewelry boxes, the smaller of which he presented to her mother. "These are for you,

Maria. Gio thought you seemed quite taken with them this afternoon, so I hope they're to your liking. But if not, they can be exchanged for something else.''

They were earrings, small and delicate, each with an oval of translucent jade poised like a teardrop above a small diamond—an exquisite gift, expensive without being ostentatious, and her mother's flush of pleasure betrayed how delighted she was to receive them.

''And this,'' he went on, opening the other box and lifting out the aquamarine pendant they'd looked at earlier, ''is for my wife because she is the only woman I know lovely enough to do it justice.''

Gabriella stared at the necklace, knowing everyone was watching her expectantly, and that she was supposed to make some sort of appropriately enthusiastic response. It was, after all, a truly magnificent piece. Instead, horrifyingly, she heard herself ask baldly, ''What's it for?''

As if it were his habit to drop priceless jewels into her lap on a weekly basis, he smiled and said, ''Why, to wear, my love. Put it on so we can see how it looks.''

''No!''

The tiny frown puckering his forehead told her she was stretching his good will past all reason. He'd made a grand gesture, to impress her parents, and now it was her turn to show suitable appreciation of the fact. ''Come on, Gabriella, it won't bite.''

''I'm not wearing...'' She backed away, semi-hypnotized by the pendant twirling and winking at her in the lamplight. ''...the right clothes. A thing like this calls for an evening gown—something rich and sumptuous.''

''It needs only you.''

He stalked her until she found herself pinioned against the arm of the sofa. His fingers brushed the back of her neck, lifted her hair, fastened the clasp of the necklace securely in place. The gold filigree chain nested lightly against her skin; the aquamarine lay heavy and cold at her throat.

He brought his hands to rest on her shoulders, turned her around to face her parents, and solicited another opinion. "What do you think, Zoltan? Will it do?"

"It is very beautiful." Her father was completely won over. There were tears in his eyes. "In the old days, our daughter would have grown up taking such lovely things for granted, but times are not as they once were, and I thank you from the bottom of my heart for restoring her to the kind of life which should have been her birthright."

"In that case, you make me doubly glad I chose it." Max paused long enough to cast a reproachful glance at Gabriella who stood there unable to dredge up so much as a semblance of enthusiasm. "Even if my wife wishes I hadn't."

"It's not that I don't appreciate the thought," she felt compelled to reply. "I just feel rather foolish wearing it when it clearly calls for a special occasion. As it is, I'm afraid it'll spend most of its time in the safe, along with my other jewelry."

Max dug in his shirt pocket and hauled out her wedding band. "That reminds me, let's put this where it belongs before I forget I have it and it winds up in the laundry! Here, my love."

He slid it over her knuckle and, if she'd allowed it, would have raised her hand to his lips and kissed it. She forestalled him, snatching her fingers away as if he'd burned them, and pulling off the ring. "No! I can't wear it!"

It was quite the wrong thing to do, and if her own common sense hadn't told her so the minute it was too late to take back the words, her mother's appalled gasp certainly conveyed the message. "Gabriella, whatever is the matter? You should be proud to wear your husband's ring!"

"I know," she said miserably. "And I would be, if only…" *If only it were for the right reasons.* But the truth was, having him put it on her finger on their wedding day had been difficult enough, knowing, as she had, that he was an unwilling groom roped into marriage because she'd thought she was expecting a baby. She could not stomach a repeat performance now when they had not even the excuse of an unplanned pregnancy to hold them together. "If only," she amended, sliding the ring back and forth over her knuckle several times to demonstrate, "it weren't so loose. But as you can see, it slips off very easily, and I'm afraid I'll lose it."

Max rolled his eyes. "What do you expect, when your idea of a square meal is a stick of celery and a grape?"

"Oh, Max, that's an exaggeration, and you know it!"

"Do I?" Once more, he appealed to her parents. "You must have noticed how she picks at her food, and you can't have missed the fact that she's dropped at least two dress sizes since you last saw her."

"But not because I've been dieting," she insisted. "It's all the traveling that's done it. Jet lag and too hectic a schedule."

*That, and eating my heart out over you! Did you ever try packing away a steak, Max, when you're hollow with misery inside and there's a permanent lump in your throat?*

"Well, your father made a good point earlier," he said. "You're not traveling now, and before you take off on your next whirlwind tour, I want to see you put back those pounds you've lost."

"As if you care!" A slip of the tongue too bitter to be contained, it was out before she could contain it.

"I care," he snapped, making no effort to hide his annoyance at her attitude. "Being seen with a wife who looks like a bone rack isn't my idea of a good time, nor do I think you're setting any sort of example to the ranks of gullible young women around the world whose ideal is to wind up looking just like you!"

"Then don't be seen with me, if it offends you so much! I've grown quite accustomed to being on my own, and you've as good as admitted you never are, so—!"

They were hurling angry words at each other, unmindful of their audience, and who was to say what irreparable damage she might have done with her last remark had Max not suddenly yanked her to him, and stopped her in midflow with a kiss which resonated throughout her body.

Arms hanging limply at her sides, she flopped against him like a rag doll, aware of his eyes glaring into hers and sparking blue flame. His mouth sealed hers so thoroughly, so crushingly, she could barely breathe and when she tried to squirm free, he nipped her lower lip just hard enough to remind her that if a contest of brute strength was what she wanted, she'd better be prepared to come out the loser.

But the really pitiful thing—the shameful, humiliating fact of the matter—was that for all her outrage, her body...and yes, her mind and heart and soul, relished every second! Just as well he had her encased in a steel grip, she thought hazily, or she'd have wound up in a mindless, soggy heap at his feet.

Sensing he'd won this latest round, Max softened the kiss. The nip became a nibble so persuasive that her lips parted and allowed his tongue to trace an apology inside her mouth, to flick and swirl against hers in tormenting reminder of what intimacy was all about.

A flash of heat, so sudden and intense it made her thighs quiver, shot to her lower abdomen and dissolved into liquid yearning. If she could have had one wish, it would have been to freeze the moment and make it last forever. To cast it like a veil over their marriage and disguise all the ugliness which kept her and Max apart.

He labored under no such fanciful delusion. With a disarming show of remorse, he pulled her into a tight hug and, resting his chin on the crown of her head, addressed her parents who sat in paralyzed fascination watching the entire performance. "I guess the secret's out and there's no use pretending it's not, so we might as well come clean. The truth is—"

Appalled that he seemed prepared to reveal their duplicity in all its shabby glory without regard for the fallout sure to follow, Gabriella struggled free. "No, Max, please! Don't do this!"

She might as well have saved her breath. "Sometimes we fight," he explained blithely, hauling her back and pressing her face into his shirtfront to silence her, "and I'm the first to admit I'm usually the one who starts it. But the truth is, I worry that Gabriella's pushing herself too hard with this modeling business. I wish she could spend more time here where she belongs, so that I can take better care of her, but that's just not feasible with her schedule."

"So you love her," her mother crooned. "We understand. And she loves you. And people who love with passion, they fight with passion."

"They make up with passion, too, Maria," he interjected quickly.

Her mother's English might not be perfect, but she understood well enough what he was implying. "So go!" she chuckled, shooing at them as if she were chasing away chickens. "It is time now to make up!"

Keeping Gabriella cinched to his side, Max picked up the bottle of cognac and offered it to her father. "Zoltan, I couldn't quite see you wearing earrings, but I remember you appreciate good brandy, so this is for you. I'm sure you'll forgive us if we leave you to enjoy it in relative peace and quiet."

Brushing aside her father's thanks, he then turned a wicked smile on Gabriella. "Now, what do you say, sweetheart? Ready to take your mom's advice?"

What choice did she have but to return his smile and go along with the suggestion? Fully aware of her parents' watchful gaze, she linked her arm around Max's waist and let him lead her toward the stairs.

## CHAPTER FIVE

THE charade came to an end the minute they reached the bedroom. "Well," he said, strolling to the window and casually unbuttoning his shirt while she wilted against the closed door, "for someone supposedly bent on preserving the myth of happy-ever-after, you certainly came close to blowing it! Care to tell me why?"

"I'm not stupid, Max," she said. "I don't know why you came home early tonight, but I do know it had nothing to do with wanting to be with me."

"As a matter of fact, it did. Looking back, I decided I was out of line in the way I handled our rather tense exchange in Gio's."

"So you thought you'd try to bribe me into forgetting about it with this?" Unclasping the pendant, she flung it at him. "No, thanks. I'm not that easily bought off."

He caught the thing and regarded her impassively. "So what do you suggest I do with it?"

Resisting the urge to give him quite graphic instructions, she said, "Give it to someone who'll appreciate it."

"You have a specific 'someone' in mind, or will just anyone do?"

"Oh, stop playing games!" she exploded. "For obscure reasons known only to you, you decided to make a few more brownie points with my parents tonight by playing the doting husband and son-in-law. Well, congratulations! You gave a near-flawless performance and they were definitely impressed. But the curtain's been rung down now and there's no one but me left in the audience, so you can drop the phony act.''

He examined the heap of gold and precious gems cradled in his palm. "There's nothing phony about this, I assure you. Would you like to see the appraisal certificate that came with it? Or the receipt, perhaps? Would *they* convince you it's the genuine article?''

"I'm not questioning the authenticity of the jewelry. It's your integrity that's on the line here, Max. Pretending we're happily married is one thing, but you take things too far when you show up loaded with expensive gifts, and start quizzing me about where I've been as if you were worried sick about me.''

"You didn't come in until after nine, and there was no sign you'd been home since morning.''

"I wasn't aware I had to report my every move to you or that I was under any sort of curfew.''

"Jeez, Gabriella, will you stop making something out of nothing, and try being reasonable for a change? Your parents are getting on, your dad had to get his doctor's permission to make the trip over here, and you have the kind of high public profile that leaves you vulnerable to every weirdo out there, so naturally I was concerned when I got home to find the place empty.''

"Rubbish! You were trying to justify your own behavior by shifting guilt on to me.''

He stared at her blankly for a moment, then said, "You know what? You're nuts! You're so caught up in your own fantasy world that you can't tell the difference between it and reality.''

"The first night I was back here, you as good as told me you're seeing someone else, and that's just plain fact, Max. Not my imagination playing tricks on me, and not another of the lies you're so quick to accuse me of manufacturing. When I confronted you about it this afternoon, you wouldn't—or couldn't—simply tell me I was worrying about nothing. So you bought me a trinket to ease your conscience.''

He dangled the pendant from his forefinger and let loose with a bellow of laughter. ''Some trinket! I know you think I'm made of money, Gabriella, but even I don't throw it around quite that casually.''

''Stop trying to change the subject,'' she fired back. ''This isn't about money—it's *never* been about money, for all that you like to think that's why I married you! It's about principles...and....'' She fought back the sob rising in her throat. Damn it, she *wouldn't* let him make her cry! She *wouldn't* back down when every instinct told her she was right!

''You're a fine one to preach to me about principles, given the way you went about snagging me in marriage!''

Beside herself, she gave in to the jealousy and doubt eating holes in her heart. ''I'm not the one with a lover waiting in the wings, either.''

''Oh, for pity's sake!'' He smacked the heel of his hand against his forehead and advanced toward her. ''Listen carefully, Gabriella, because I'm going to say this as plainly as I know how, and I'm only going to say it once. *There is no other woman*...not anymore.''

At his denial, initially so clean and convincing, a huge uprush of hope rose inside her, only to be smashed into oblivion by the squalid little qualification he tacked on at the end.

''But there was,'' she mourned on a fragile breath, the pain of his admission so acute that her words were barely audible. Only a sadist would withdraw the knife from a person's heart for the pure pleasure of plunging it in more deeply a second time!

"Yes." Recognizing the wound he'd inflicted, he caught her hands in his. "But not in the way you think. When it came right down to breaking my marriage vows..." He lifted his shoulders in a mystified shrug. "I couldn't do it."

She should have taken comfort wherever it was to be found, but the perverse need to punish herself further made her ask, "Are you saying you've never kissed her?"

He hesitated, his eyes scouring her face, his own expression a mixture of regret and amusement. "Oh, I've kissed her," he finally admitted, cupping her face in his hands and bringing his mouth so close to hers that she could almost taste it. "But never like this."

She had thought nothing could equal the upheaval he'd created with his earlier kiss, put on for her parents' benefit. She had thought nothing could ever erase the devastation of hearing him concede he'd turned for solace to someone else. But the way he settled his mouth on hers, unprompted by obligation or duty, swept aside all the previous hurts. All at once, the sincerity of the here and now were all that counted.

"You're a thorn in my side, Gabriella," he murmured, the words grazing her lips. "I would prefer to ignore you...forget I ever met you...but even when you're half a world away, I'm never really free of you."

"And you hate me for that," she whispered without any real conviction.

"You irritate the hell out of me." His mouth drifted to her jaw and down the side of her neck, stitching expert little kisses between each word.

"I know," she sighed, aware in a distant corner of her mind that his hands had strayed down past her waist and were tracing delectable patterns over her hips.

If she had an ounce of moral fiber, she'd put an end to

his seduction. What kind of woman settled for the transient pleasure of the moment when the past was riddled with one betrayal after another, and the future too uncertain to contemplate?

Yet, what right had she to object, when she herself had thrust aside the open front of his shirt and was conducting an uninvited tour of the planes of his chest? How warm and solid he was; how deeply, dearly familiar!

He reached behind her to pull down the zipper on her dress. "You infuriate me."

"At least I haven't kissed another man since I married you." Reaching up, she punished his transgression by nipping lightly at the smooth, tanned skin of his shoulder.

He let out a faint gasp.

Annoyance? Pleasure? She thought the latter.

"You're never going to let me forget that, are you?" He'd inched her dress off her shoulders. It slithered the length of her body and fell with a rustling sigh around her ankles. She heard the soft click of her bra being undone. A cool draft of night air whispered over her skin except where his hands warmed her bare breasts. "You're going to blackmail me with it for the rest of my life."

"That shouldn't come as any great surprise. You persist in believing I'm a conniving witch out to trick you at every turn." Her throat closed over the accusation as he took her nipple in his mouth. Could he tell that each time his tongue circled her flesh, a tiny paroxysm of sensation throbbed deep within her? Did he know she was wet with wanting him?

"But you *did* trick me," he said, dropping to his knees and leaving the damp imprint of his kisses against the thin silk of her panties. "You told me my baby was in *here*."

She was aching; shuddering all over. Knotting her fingers in his hair, she pressed her knees together to keep herself upright. "I thought it was. My period was late and I panicked."

"You let me think other men had touched you—*here.*"

Sweet heaven, he had cupped his hand over the drenched patch of fabric between her legs! He knew how eager she was for him; how incapable of pretending indifference to his encroachment. His fingers were inching inside her panties. Inside *her,* and moving with such deft purpose, she was about to shatter into a million pieces!

A hoarse cry caught in her throat and she collapsed against him. As if she weighed no more than a feather, he tipped her over his shoulder and rose to his feet. The room swam past in a blur as he strode to the bed and dropped her there, just carelessly enough that she bounced gently on the mattress.

He turned on the bedside lamp and leaned over her, his eyes glittering. "You're not lying now, though, are you, Gabriella? You want to make love, don't you?"

*Beast!* He already knew the answer, but he was going to make her beg anyway! "I don't really care one way or the other," she said weakly and closed her eyes.

"Look at me when you say that."

Mesmerized, she obeyed. When he saw that he had her unblinking attention, he reached for his belt. The buckle glimmered in the lamplight. He unsnapped the waist of his jeans, and slowly opened the fly. "Do you still not care?"

She bit her lip and refused to answer.

He smiled grimly. "You want to touch me, don't you, my love?"

"No," she whimpered, even as her hand stole out to shape him. He was hard, powerful; throbbing with suppressed energy and life.

"Shall I leave you then, and go take a cold shower?"

*"No!"* Driven past all reason, she lunged at him and tore frenziedly at the blue jeans. He wore jockey shorts underneath, dazzling white against the dark tan of his thighs. And oh, such thighs they were, tapering from his hips in one long, smooth sweep of muscled flesh!

"Help me!" she implored, struggling with the unyielding denim and quite beside herself. She wouldn't settle for a hurried, halfhearted coupling, not after all those days and nights of unanswered yearning! "You've got me where you want me—naked and vulnerable. I want to see all of you, as well."

Pinning her in a searing, heavy-lidded gaze, he shucked off what remained of his clothes and stalked her across the bed with the unhurried grace of a lion moving in for an easy kill.

When at last he was close enough that his breath ruffled her hair, he growled, "Not quite naked, my love," and stripped off her panties, then pushed her back against the pillows and went about the business of reacquainting himself with her body, touching her first with his hands, and then with his mouth.

He kissed her eyes and her throat; her elbows, her feet, each separate vertebra in her spine. And when every other inch of her had received its benediction and was humming with pleasure, he pushed apart her knees and touched his tongue to her most secret and sensitive flesh.

He'd brought her to climax before, but never so swiftly or so savagely. She tried to resist it, to tame it. But her body had gone too long without him and responded with the avid greed of a starving thing. Racked by spasm after spasm, she clung to him, sobbing his name.

As the tremors faded to a sweet echo, he sank down beside her and went to take her in his arms. But seeing the tears tracking down her face, he rose up again on one elbow and said ruefully, "Heck, Gabriella, it seems no matter how hard I try to please you, all I ever do is make you cry."

She uttered a shaky laugh, and ran her hands over his torso, loving the feel of him, all muscle overlaid by smooth, olive-tinted skin. "You took me by surprise, that's all."

"Keep up what you're doing, and you'll be surprised all over again," he warned her. "You're wandering into dangerous territory, sweetheart, so unless you're prepared to deal with the consequences, better keep your hands to yourself."

"Not a chance," she said, pressing him back against the mattress. "You've had your fun. Now it's my turn."

The hint of complacency in his smile suggested he thought there was little chance she could wreak on him anything approaching the havoc he'd brought to her, but as she inched her way down his chest, she heard the uneven thump of his heart and knew he wasn't nearly as much in control as he'd like her to believe.

"Is this what you meant, when you asked me if I wanted to touch you?" she whispered, closing her fingers possessively around the straining evidence of his arousal.

He inhaled sharply.

Encouraged to boldness, she inquired huskily, "Or is this more what you had in mind?"

At the brush of her lips, a groan escaped him. "Woman," he ground out, "you're playing with fire."

Undeterred, she swept her mouth over him again, branding him with hot, impassioned kisses. Being together with him like this was a gift from the gods she did not intend to waste. The next time he was tempted to stray, she wanted hers to be the touch he'd yearn for, hers the face to haunt him in the night.

He might resent her until the day he died, but like it or not, *she* was his wife, and for all that she'd thought divorce was her only option, she knew now that she would not easily relinquish the role to someone else. Suddenly, *For better or for worse, till death us do part* assumed new and powerful meaning.

"Gabriella…!" Her name emerged on a long, unsteady breath. Gripping her shoulders, he hauled her up beside him again, rolled her onto her back, and knelt astride her. His forehead gleamed with sweat. A pulse raced at the corner of his jaw, keeping pace with the speeding rush of her own heart. His voice rough with passion, he said, "Enough! I want to be inside you when I come."

"Yes," she sighed dreamily, her entire body vibrating with anticipation as he nudged apart her thighs. And then the long, lonely waiting was over. He was where he belonged and for once happy to be there…velvet sheathed in satin…and they were moving together in remembered rhythm. Rediscovering each other. Turning painful past knowledge into beautiful, shimmering new experiences. Holding on to each other as the tempo increased and they tried to outrace the roaring tide gathering force and threatening to tip them, end over end, into extinction.

It was splendor enough, more than she'd dared dream about, and she would not have asked for more. But just as he lost the battle for supremacy and his seed spilled hotly within her, he gave her one last gift—words dredged up from the darkest depths of his soul, tortured and almost indistinguishable.

"Darling!" he muttered feverishly, crushing her to him. "Beloved!"

Impossible words. She could not have heard him correctly.

Lifting her hand, she stroked the hair from his brow. "What did you say, Max?"

He let out an exhausted sigh and rolled to his side, his body still fused with hers. "Hush. It was nothing."

"You called me 'darling.'"

"Uh-uh. 'Devil', more like it."

"And 'beloved.'"

"Let it go, Gabriella." He flopped onto his back and tucked her head into the crook of his shoulder.

"I can't," she cried, bereft of his warmth and the sweet sense of completion that came of having him buried inside her. "What just happened...didn't it mean *anything* to you?"

"What do you think?"

"That it was beautiful. That for the first time ever, neither of us was using the other. Instead, we gave to one another, and in doing so, we truly did *make love*." She stopped and drew in a tormented breath. "Am I wrong?"

He debated the question so long that she found herself biting her lip to keep it from trembling. *Please*, she begged him silently, *please don't turn what we just shared into something cheap and tawdry!*

"You're not wrong," he finally admitted. "The question is, where does that leave us?"

"We're husband and wife, Max. Can't we take it from there and try to make something worthwhile of our marriage?"

"Being legally bound to each other no more makes for marriage than great sex does. Face it, Gabriella, your life isn't with me, it's wherever your work takes you, be it Rome or Paris or Buenos Aires."

"If you asked me to, I would give it all up in a heartbeat."

"In exchange for what? Being unhappy, the way you

were before you made a new life for yourself away from me?''

"I could be very happy with you, if you'd let me," she said urgently. "Will you do that, Max? Will you give us another chance?''

"I'm tempted, I admit." He looked at her long and seriously before continuing, "Will you settle for giving it a trial run on the understanding that, after your parents leave, we'll take an honest look at where we stand and if we find it isn't working out, we'll agree to part without recrimination or blame on either part?''

*It will work out!* she promised him silently. "Agreed.''

"Not so fast. You also have to promise me—''

"Anything!" she cried softly, the fulfillment of all her hopes and dreams hanging by a thread.

"There'll be no more lies. And I'm not just talking about lying to each other. We've got to stop fooling ourselves, Gabriella. Regardless of where it might lead, I want your promise that you'll assess *us* honestly. No skating over the bits you don't like, no pretending that if you ignore them, the problems will go away. Otherwise, we don't have a snowball's chance in hell of repairing what's broken between us.''

Solemnly, she drew a cross over her heart. "I give you my word. And, Max, one more thing...''

"What now?''

She picked up the necklace from the bedside table where Max had tossed it, and fastened it around her throat again. "Thank you for this. I love it.''

"Good. Because I pressured Gio into staying late at the shop and taking some of the links out of the chain so it would fit properly." He leaned over and switched off the bedside lamp. "If you behave yourself, I might have him make up something from the left-over diamonds and gold.''

"I don't need anything else," she whispered. "What you've given me just now, here in this room, is worth more to me than all the diamonds and gold in the world."

He reached for her in the dark. "Want to know the best part about tonight?" he said, his voice rough with renewed passion. "It isn't over yet."

It was after ten when she opened her eyes the next morning. "You should have woken me sooner," she scolded her mother whom she found snipping dead roses from the climber on the terrace while her father put himself through his usual twenty laps in the pool. "Imagine letting me sleep most of the morning away when you're already halfway through your time here!"

Her mother uncovered a dish of berries and cream waiting on the patio table. "Your man said not to disturb you. And he is right. You're worn to skin and bone, my daughter. You need rest and good food. So, sit and eat, and I will make eggs the way you used to like them, with fresh rolls and sweet butter."

"No eggs, Mama, thank you. Fruit and a roll will be enough, though I'd love a cup of coffee as well, if you'll join me."

Humming under her breath, her mother bustled inside the penthouse. Overhead, seagulls glided across a calm blue midsummer sky. A rose in a bud vase in the middle of the table glowed deep gold in the sunlight. Down in the bay, a boat drifted slowly under sail, headed for the open sea.

*Paradise!* Gabriella thought, stretching lazily and savoring every tiny body ache for the reminder it brought of the night just past. She closed her eyes, the better to review the film unwinding in her mind—of waking somewhere around two in the morning, with the moon casting long pewter shadows over Max's limbs entwined with hers; of the sandpaper burn of his beard against her skin, the thrilling crescendo to their lovemaking, so vivid in recall that a tremor of sensation spiraled through her womb. Of the musky scent of afterward, deeply private, intensely intimate, and the warm, secure feel of her husband's arms folded around her in sleep.

Yes, paradise indeed—or a miracle so impossible that she found herself wondering if it had all been just a dream. Would he come home later and look at her from cold, empty eyes? Would his kiss once again be only a parody of the real thing?

Suddenly, she needed to hear his voice, to hear him turn her name into an embrace, the way he had in the quiet hours before the dawn—*Gabri...ell...a!*

A remote phone lay on the table, preprogrammed with his office number. It rang twice before a woman answered. "Willow McHenry," she purred.

"I...um, that is, I thought I'd dialed..." Annoyed to find herself stumbling over her words, Gabriella sat up straight and began again. "Is this Max Logan's office?"

"It is."

"Then may I speak to him, please?"

"I'm afraid Mr. Logan's unavailable at the moment. I'll be happy to relay a message to him."

If he was unavailable, why could she hear his voice quite plainly in the background? "No," Gabriella said firmly. "I wish to speak to him in person."

There was a muffled pause, the kind which comes from a hand being placed over a receiver to disguise the conversation taking place at the other end. Finally, her tone suggesting that importuning Mr. Logan was no one's prerogative but hers, Willow McHenry came back on the line to inquire, "Who may I say is calling?"

Who? The woman he made love to all last night, that's *who!* "His wife," Gabriella said.

Another pause, lasting perhaps five seconds or more, and so utterly silent this time that there was no question of any conversation taking place at the other end of the line. Gabriella flinched as the phone smacked against some hard surface, then Max's voice came on the line, not as loverlike as she'd have preferred, but not chillingly neutral, either. "Hi, Gabriella. What's up?"

"Well, I am—finally," she said with a laugh. "But I missed saying goodbye to you this morning."

"You were sleeping so soundly, I thought it best not to wake you."

In the background, a door closed sharply.

"I wish you had."

He waited a moment before replying, and there was answering laughter in his voice when he said, "I had a conference call scheduled for eight o'clock and didn't want to risk being late."

"I wouldn't have kept you very long."

"Yes, you would, you insatiable wench. We'd likely still be rolling between the sheets."

She turned liquid with pleasure. "I miss you. Come home early, will you?"

"As soon as I can. I'll take us all out for dinner. Choose some place nice outside town that you think your folks might enjoy seeing, and make a reservation for eight."

Smiling, he hung up the phone.

"Well," Willow said from the other end of the room, "aren't you the dutiful husband all of a sudden!"

He cast her a sideways glance before turning his attention to the contract lying on his desk. "I think we both know that's been my role all along."

"Not quite," she said. "I remember an occasion when you came very close to forgetting you even had a wife."

His hand stilled on the pages he'd been leafing through. "Let's not rake up the past, Willow," he said flatly. "We were both at a low point in our lives, but we managed to get past it without hurting anyone."

"You might have, Max," she said, coming to face him across the desk, "but don't presume to know how I felt."

He didn't like the tone of the conversation; he liked even less the brittle tone in her voice. "We're talking about a couple of kisses one night, eight months ago," he said, staring her straight in the eye. "I thought we'd both moved on since then. But if you find you haven't, or can't, I'll be happy to arrange a transfer to another department, or give you a reference, if you prefer to move to another company."

"No." She flashed him a brilliant smile. "You're quite right, we *have* moved on. I'm involved with someone else and you're…still married."

"Yes," he said. "And the next time my wife phones, put her call through right away. I'm never too busy to talk to her."

"Of course. She has a lovely voice, by the way. Charmingly young and foreign. Naive, almost, which I wouldn't have expected from someone so used to public exposure." She scooped up the letters she'd left for him to sign and made for the door connecting their two offices. "Oh, a couple of things I should mention before I forget. First, that person from the local TV station called again yesterday, wanting to set up an interview with you. What shall I tell him?"

"Anything, as long as I don't have to go in front of the camera. That's my wife's forte, not mine."

"All right. I'll suggest they line something up with her instead."

"Sure, as long as she's agreeable."

"And the Overseas Development Dinner's next Thursday. Since you're almost certain to win an award, shall I order extra tickets for your wife and her parents?"

"It hadn't occurred to me before, but now that you mention it, yes, do. I think they'd enjoy themselves."

"Fine." She bathed him in another smile and was gone.

He remained standing behind the desk, though, uneasiness tugging at his gut—with a dollop of guilt thrown in for good measure.

It had started out innocently enough with Willow: working late, and sharing a take-out dinner while they raced to complete a deal on time; lunch to celebrate final approval on a building site or a five-star rating on the latest hotel; flowers delivered to her at home in recognition of the extra hours she pulled down when he was out of town; a token gift to go with the annual bonus at Christmas; a friendly kiss at the office party.

He should have left it that. But then, there'd been the night at the penthouse, a couple of glasses of wine too many, an ill-advised attempt to start an affair which fizzled before it properly began, and that had been it. As far as he was concerned, their relationship had been strictly confined to business ever since.

If anyone had asked him yesterday, he'd have said with absolute certainty that she felt the same way. She was too smart and attractive to hanker after a married man when there were any number of eligible guys available. And too ambitious to jeopardize a job that paid handsomely and offered the kind of perks that went along with being chief assistant to the company boss.

Today, he wasn't so sure. There'd been something in her voice, something in the way her expression closed up when he'd suggested she might be happier working for someone else. He'd been reminded of a dog prepared to fight to the death defending its territory all the time it was wagging its tail in a show of apparent friendliness.

Scowling, he paced to the window, all too aware of the potential fallout if he didn't handle the situation delicately. Given the turn of events with Gabriella, the ideal solution would be to transfer Willow, preferably to one of the overseas branches. But given today's climate in the work place, he knew well enough he'd leave himself wide open to a suit of sexual harassment if he tried to force the issue. The best he could do was keep their relationship thoroughly professional, and hope like hell that she'd show up one day soon with a ring on her finger, and a letter of resignation in her hand.

The damnable thing was, a week ago he hadn't much cared which way it went. She could accept the status quo, or she could leave. But then, a week ago, he'd had nothing to lose if she stayed. The last thing he'd expected was that his marriage which had seemed doomed from the start, might be worth saving, after all.

# CHAPTER SIX

GABRIELLA had made an eight o'clock reservation at a restaurant in White Rock, a residential community famous for its beaches and spectaculars views, some forty-five-minute drive south of the city. The rush-hour traffic was long over by then and he'd normally have made it out there with time to spare. Coming home to find her all rosy from the shower and wearing only a silk camisole and bikini panties, though, threw the schedule seriously off track.

Leaving her parents happily sipping dry sherry downstairs, Max locked the bedroom door behind him and dedicated himself to stripping his wife naked and pulling her back into the shower—this time, with him.

"We'll be late," she said, wrapping her long golden legs around his waist. "Max, they won't hold our...table if we're...ah...!"

Her protest, halfhearted to begin with, died as he parted the sleek folds of her flesh and slid inside her. He'd have preferred to take her at leisure, to track the curls of steam writhing around the tips of her breasts. To watch the flush riding up her neck as he edged her closer to the brink of orgasm. He'd have liked to taste the lush ripeness of her mouth and muffle her little cries of delirium as she convulsed helplessly around him.

But almost immediately, the ache lurking all day in his lower belly tightened excruciatingly, and before he could help himself, he had her cushioned between him and the glass wall of the shower stall, the pulsing urgency gushed free, and he was left drained and gasping.

"That's what comes of being celibate too long," he panted ruefully, dropping his forehead to hers. "Now that you've reminded me what I've been missing all these months, I can't hold out long enough to make it worth your while."

But the unfocused dreaminess in her eyes put the lie to his allegation as surely as the diminishing contractions clenching her body. "Don't say that!" she cried, her breath sweet against his mouth. "It was—*you* are..." Her eyelids drooped fetchingly. "...out of this world!"

Reluctantly, he set her back on her feet and lathered a sponge. "Much more of that kind of ego-stroking and I'll be fueled up and ready to go another round—which wouldn't be such a bad thing if it weren't that you can't afford to miss a meal. Turn around, sweetheart, and I'll scrub your back."

She was as beautiful from behind as she was in front. Her spine ran straight and delicate, bisecting her in perfect symmetry from her tail bone to her nape. Her ribs, too thin still but elegantly fashioned, tapered to the kind of narrow waist which women used to lace themselves into steel corsets to achieve. As for her hips...oh, brother! Dangerous territory and not a good idea to let his thoughts linger there!

"You're done," he said, sounding as if he'd just swallowed a pail of coarse sand.

Eyes and smile alight with mischief, she pivoted to face him and made a grab for the sponge. "I'll be happy to return the favor, if you like."

He slid open the shower door and practically shoved her out of the stall. "Get yourself dressed and downstairs before your folks come looking for us, wenchkin! The sherry decanter must be empty by now.''

It wasn't. Not even close. But her parents had enjoyed the small amount they'd consumed. Either that, or they owed their rosy glow to whatever Gabriella was telling them when Max joined them in the living room, ten minutes later.

''Don't be too forthcoming about the way things seem to be turning around with you and me,'' he warned her quietly, as they waited in the building's main foyer for his car to be brought up from the garage. ''We don't know ourselves how well it's going to work and it wouldn't be fair to raise their hopes needlessly if, at the end of it all, we decide to call the marriage quits.''

She looked a little hurt, which worried him. Sure, they were about as compatible as any couple could be when it came to sex—they always had been, even when things were at their worst. But she had to know they couldn't predicate the future on a truce which had yet to survive the light of two days, let alone two weeks.

''I haven't mentioned a word,'' she said. ''Not that it would make any difference if I had. They're already convinced we're a match made in heaven. I'm just hoping they're right.''

He squeezed her hand. ''It's early days still is all I'm saying.''

''I know.'' Her mouth drooped a bit, then turned up in the smile the rest of the world knew so well. Blinding. Stunning. ''But I'll take my chances. We've been given a second chance, and that's more than I ever expected.''

''You look lovely, you know that?'' He fingered the collar of the little linen jacket she wore. ''I'll be the envy of every other man in the restaurant.''

He wasn't far wrong. From the commotion her arrival

caused, she was obviously recognized. Conversation dribbled to a halt. Heads swivelled to watch as the maître d' did a double take, nearly tripped over backwards bowing her to their table, and just about wet his drawers when she began discussing the menu with him in fluent French.

Hiding his grin behind the wine list, Max said under his breath, ''You planning to talk dirty like that to me in bed tonight, dear heart?''

Hidden by the tablecloth, she walked her fingers from his knee and all the way up his inner thigh to the danger zone. ''I'll do better than talk,'' she promised him.

He laughed, not only because her audacity amused him, but because…damn it, she made him happy.

How had it happened? When they'd first married, he'd been so bloody angry that, once his pride had adjusted to her walking out on him, he'd embraced the peace she left behind. What others might have called lonely and boring, he'd viewed as a return to bachelor contentment. Any time he'd found himself inclined to wonder about her—even to miss her—all he'd had to do to snap out of it was think back to the emotional storms and manipulations which were her trademark, and count his blessings at being rid of her.

Yet here she was again, creating a different kind of upheaval, but an upheaval nevertheless, and he felt alive for the first time in over a year. ''I'm starting out with oysters on the half shell,'' he told her, clamping his hand over hers before she got them both thrown out on their ears for lewd behavior in a public place. ''I get the feeling I'm going to need them.''

Another two days went by before the glow began to wear off. Then, early on the third morning, a Friday, the phone rang.

"Mrs. Logan? It's Willow McHenry, Max's executive assistant."

Even before the woman identified herself, Gabriella recognized her voice. Noticed, too, the possessive way she wrapped her mouth around Max's name.

"I'm calling to arrange a time for your interview."

Gabriella stared at the phone. "I beg your pardon?"

"Your television appearance, Mrs. Logan. Max has already given it the go-ahead in the hopes that it will satisfy the media's preoccupation with your visit. Your being in town is causing such a stir, and he so dislikes being flung in the spotlight, as I expect you know." She allowed a pregnant pause to spin out. "Or perhaps you don't. In any event, this is something he and I have discussed at length—the interview idea, that is. Am I to assume that he forgot to mention it to you?"

"We talked about my arrival not exactly going unnoticed by the press, but—"

She might as well have saved her breath. Willow McHenry tromped right over her reply as if it amounted to yet one more tiny inconvenience in the lives of the rich and powerful, and continued smoothly, "Small wonder if he overlooked it, given how very busy he is, but that's what he pays me to do—take care of the minor details he doesn't have time for."

Willow McHenry, Gabriella decided, came across as a tigress of a woman, formidably competent and immovably certain of her place in the greater order of things. A future CEO in her own right, she was most likely tall and frighteningly attractive, probably wore a lot of black, with plum-red lipstick and nail lacquer for contrast—and was so ultra chic and efficient that lesser mortals cringed in her presence!

Unaware of the impact she'd made, Willow forged

ahead. "I've suggested to the person who'll be conducting the interview that the taping take place at the penthouse, an idea which she quite likes."

Finally finding her voice again, Gabriella said, "I'm not at all sure that I do. My home is private and I prefer to keep it that way."

Another tiny paused ensued. "But Max's living room is so elegant—quite beyond anything you'd find in a television studio, and the view from the terrace is breathtaking. If you're concerned about having to prepare for the event, I'll be there ahead of time to run interference and make sure you're inconvenienced as little as possible. All you need to do is look ravishing, which is something you're quite used to and which will, I'm sure, require no effort at all."

"Thank you—I think."

The irony was lost on Willow. "Mrs. Logan, we need to settle on the date. How's your calendar looking for Tuesday?"

"I'll have to check with my husband. My parents are visiting from overseas and we might have other plans."

"Not for Tuesday you won't. Max is flying to New Mexico on Monday and won't be back until Wednesday. And while we're talking dates, there's the Overseas Development Awards Dinner on Thursday—I've arranged extra tickets for you and your guests, by the way—so how about I pencil you in for ten o'clock Tuesday morning? Will that give you enough time to get yourself dressed and ready?"

It was all Gabriella could do not to come back with, *I'm a model, not a moron, I've been dressing myself since I turned five, and I've yet to show up in mismatched shoes!* "I think I might be able to manage that," she said from between clenched teeth.

"Then it's arranged. I've already run the time past the studio crew and they're available. I'll see you on Tuesday around half-past nine."

After dinner that evening, Max suggested he and Gabriella take a stroll through the park, just the two of them. "I'm enjoying your folks' company," he said, linking her fingers in his and leading her along a deserted path shaded by Japanese maples, "but I think it's important for you and me to spend time alone together."

"We're by ourselves every night in bed."

"I know!" He leered at her disarmingly. "But we just keep covering the same old ground in there! Not that I'm complaining, you understand, but if we're serious about trying to make this marriage work, we need to put it to the test in other areas, as well." He swung their joined hands back and forth. "For instance, I thought you seemed a bit preoccupied at dinner tonight. Is something wrong?"

Should she tell him, or would it be more prudent to push aside the misgivings which had dogged her ever since the conversation with Willow McHenry?

Catching her hesitation, he pulled her to a stop and forced her to look him in the eye. "Okay, you just answered my question. What's up?"

"I haven't said a word!"

"You don't have to. Something's bugging you and I want to know what it is. Come *on*, Gabriella, this is exactly the sort of thing I'm talking about! You can't go sweeping stuff under the carpet and hope it'll go away, because we both know that's not how marriage works. So spit it out, whatever it is, and let's deal with it."

"All right. Your assistant phoned me this morning."

"Yeah?" Was it her imagination, or did his gaze become a little less direct, a little more guarded? "What did she want?"

"It seems the two of you decided I should be interviewed on television."

"Oh, *that!*" He made a wry face. "I wouldn't put it in quite those words, but she was basically correct."

"Max, why would you give permission for something like that without asking me first?"

"Honey, you're already headline news around here— *World Famous Model Comes Home,* and all that jazz. Because the penthouse isn't listed in the phone book, you've been spared any personal harassment, but the endless calls Willow's had to field at the office on your behalf have really cut into the time she'd allocated for other things."

Gabriella could well imagine how the super-efficient Ms. McHenry would resent that! Still, "I wish you'd discussed it with me before you went ahead. My reasons for being here are private, and I'm not about to air them in public."

Laughing, he slung a casual arm around her shoulder and resumed walking. "Don't tell me you're nervous in front of a camera! If anyone can handle herself, you certainly can."

"It's not that so much as..." She gnawed the inside of her cheek, uncertain of the wisdom of airing her real concern.

"What? Come on, sweetheart, stop looking like Bo Peep about to be attacked by the spider! Tell me what's really troubling you."

How could she say, *We've never met, but I sense your assistant doesn't like me any more than I'm inclined to like her—or the fact that she seems to be very familiar with the layout of our home!*

She couldn't, it was as simple as that. Their truce was

too new, too fragile. So she settled for a safer middle ground. "Okay, it's the way I've been swept into this. I don't mind telling you, I find Ms. McHenry rather over-powering."

"She does come on a bit strong at times, but she means well and she's very efficient. She'll see to it that everything runs like clockwork."

"She's also very…protective of you." Yes! *Protective* was a much wiser choice than *possessive* which was the word she'd have preferred to use. "I got the distinct impression that she resents me. She as good as said my being here was interfering with your work."

"Then she was out of line and I'll speak to her. It won't happen again."

Gabriella flung him a sideways glance. Something—a certain tension threading his voice, and the same rare uneasiness in his manner which she'd seen her first night back when the subject of marital fidelity had come up for discussion—set off warning bells and forced her to confront the suspicion she'd tried desperately hard to ignore. *Willow McHenry was the woman who'd almost made him forget his wedding vows!*

"Is she right, Max?" she asked him quietly. "Do you wish I'd stayed away?"

"Do you think I'd have agreed to try to revive our marriage, if that were the case?"

It was still there, that twinge of disquiet he couldn't quite suppress.

*Say "no", and make light of the whole business. Change the subject. Don't give him grounds to accuse you of trying to keep him on a leash like a pet dog, the way he did when you were first married and couldn't bear to be apart from him!*

"She sounded very sure of her facts."

"What about what I'm telling you? Shouldn't that count for more?"

"It does," she said, wishing she'd kept her mouth shut. Even if Willow McHenry was the other woman, he'd told Gabriella nothing had really happened beyond kissing. "Of course it does."

Bracing his hands on her shoulders, he held her at arm's length. "I hope so. Because this attempt at a reconciliation is about us—you and me—laying our hearts on the line and daring to take each other on trust. No one else comes into the mix, Gabriella. And if you find yourself questioning that—"

"I'm not," she cried, turning her head to press a kiss to his hand. "I do trust you, Max."

He regarded her soberly. "I hope so," he said.

But the doubts she heard in his voice found an answering echo in her heart. Try as she might, she couldn't shake the feeling that Willow remained a threat, whether or not Max realized it. And because of that, Gabriella's bright hopes no longer shone with untarnished brilliance.

Nor, it appeared, did his. He didn't hold her hand again, and the easy camaraderie they'd known when they started out dwindled into strained silence. He strode back to the penthouse immersed in his own thoughts and seemed almost to have forgotten she was there beside him.

*Why? Because he was thinking about Willow whose self-confidence was such that she'd never known a moment's uncertainty in her life? Was he wishing he was with her, instead of his neurotic wife?*

The questions nagged at her unmercifully.

She and Max didn't make love that night. They lay side by side, not touching, the unacknowledged rift between them slight and intangible as a moonbeam. He fell asleep before she did. In the glow of city lights infiltrating the bedroom, she could see the steady rise and fall of his chest, the dark blur of his head against the pillows.

He was close enough that she could feel the warmth of his skin, yet so far removed that a million miles of loneliness separated them. It was her fault. She should not have brought the ghosts out into the open. They belonged in the shadows.

Miserably, she curled up on her side away from him, and forced herself to close her eyes and not...*not*...give way to the gremlins of uncertainty gnawing at the edges of her mind. *He had said it was over and he would never deceive her! It was not his style.*

She slept poorly, chased by uneasy dreams. Then, just as the sky began to lighten, she awoke to find his body pressed against hers, hard and ready. Without a word, she turned into his arms and opened herself to him.

They fused with a passion touched by desperation. Time and again he tormented her, withdrawing almost completely and then, when she was ready to weep with need, plunging deep within her, rapidly, fiercely, as if he were seeking to take hold of her soul. "I missed you last night," he told her hoarsely, between thrusts. "Don't let silly unfounded fears come between us like that again."

The woman who rang the doorbell at precisely nine-thirty on the morning of the interview could not possibly be Willow McHenry, Gabriella decided, barely masking her surprise. There were no long red fingernails, no hard unsmiling mouth, no dark hair secured in a sleek French twist.

This woman was shorter than Gabriella by a good six inches, with a sweetly rounded body, warm brown eyes and gleaming light brown hair curling softly around her face. She wore a buttery-yellow linen suit with a skirt which came to just below her knees, and sensibly stylish sandals with a bit of a wedge heel. Her nose was slightly freckled, her mouth rather full and defined by tawny lip gloss, her smile wide and generous. Not a beauty, by any means, but definitely pretty—and still frighteningly capable.

"Good morning, Mrs. Logan, I'm Willow, I see you're ready, that's good," she rattled off, breezing into the penthouse with an armful of creamy-pink roses and a large straw bag extravagantly embroidered with bright orange raffia marigolds.

Gabriella couldn't take her eyes off the bag. She'd expected an alligator briefcase. And very high heels.

"We'll need coffee," Willow declared, making a bee-line for the kitchen.

"I'll make some," Gabriella offered, trailing after her in stunned amazement. This woman a marriage wrecker? Absurd! She was too...wholesome.

"No need," Willow warbled. "I came prepared. I'll just arrange the roses before I do anything else."

"I already have flowers—"

"Well, you know what they say. You can never have too many flowers or be too thin, though I'd say you're coming pretty close to disproving the latter! You're so slender, a person could almost snap you in half with her bare hands."

"I'll go find you a vase," Gabriella said, trying not to back away too hastily. Willow McHenry's hands were as capable as the rest of her, and looked more than equal to the task.

"I'll do it. Max made it very clear that you're not to be put to any extra trouble, so please just sit and relax— on the terrace would be best, so that you're not in the way while the camera crew sets up. You look lovely, by the way. Your photos don't begin to do you justice." She pulled open the door to a corner cupboard and peered inside, rising up on her toes to gain a better view. "What happened to the vases which used to be in here?"

"I moved them," Gabriella said, a prickle of annoyance riding up her spine. Whose kitchen was it, anyway?

"I see. In that case, if you'd be so kind…?" Willow's raised eyebrows and upturned palms spoke volumes, but just in case her request wasn't coming across clearly enough, she followed up with, "Where did you put them, dear?"

"In the storage room."

"Ah!" She bustled unerringly across the foyer to the little room under the stairs.

Gabriella watched in numb fascination and reminded herself that Max had almost missed his flight to New Mexico the day before, because he hadn't been able to tear himself away from her. *That* was the important thing, not the proprietary way his assistant had swept in and usurped the role of lady of the house!

"I brought a list of questions you're likely to be asked," Willow announced, reappearing with a Waterford rose bowl and tall antique urn. She set them down on the counter and reached for a folder in the straw bag. "Here they are. Why don't you go look them over and leave me to take care of things in here? As soon as it's brewed, I'll bring you some coffee. Are your parents here, by the way?"

"Yes," Gabriella said. "They're enjoying the morning sun on the terrace."

"How sweet. You must introduce them to me when I have a moment."

She reached into the bag again, and brought out a sack of coffee beans, a carton of light cream, and a small round cake tin with a picture of the late Princess Diana on the lid. "Oatmeal cookies," she explained, noticing Gabriella's curious glance. "I baked them myself, just this morning."

*You probably spin your own knitting wool and do prize-winning petit point, too!* Gabriella thought uncharitably, and hurriedly left the room, more annoyed with herself than the amazing Ms. McHenry.

*I'll phone you every night,* Max had promised, before he'd dashed through the departure gate at the airport. *Honey, I'm sorry to be taking off like this, but when Willow set up this meeting, she wasn't aware you and your folks would be here, and it was too late to change things by the time I realized the conflict.*

Ha! Gabriella suspected Willow had been fully aware, but what she didn't know was that Max had phoned his wife three times last night, and told her he missed her so much he didn't think he could hold out until Wednesday and was trying to wind up his business a day early so that they didn't have to wait until tomorrow to be together again.

So she had no reason to feel threatened. No reason at all. Let Willow do her worst. When it came right down to it, the only person truly capable of undermining her confidence was Gabriella herself.

Burying a sigh, she wandered into the living room and picked up the photograph of her and Max on their wedding day. She'd worn her grandmother's bridal veil and a dress embroidered with seed pearls. Max had worn a morning suit, and the same grim expression that had transformed his face the day he'd learned she was pregnant...

*"You're what?"* he'd roared in subdued horror, when she told him the news.

They'd been sitting outside at Gerbaud's, Budapest's

most famous and elegant coffeehouse, and patrons at nearby tables had turned their heads to discover who was causing such an untoward commotion.

Gabriella had cringed, and repeated the news in a whisper. "I'm going to have a...baby."

"And you're saying it's mine?" He'd waved the question aside and regarded her from haunted eyes. "No, don't answer that. Who else's could it be?"

"I'm sorry, Max," she'd said in the same low voice. "I know this wasn't part of your plan."

"Was it part of yours?" he'd flung at her contemptuously.

"Of course not! I had no idea—"

"Right! You just happened to climb into bed with me when you were at your most fertile!"

His chest had risen in a massive sigh. "Well, never let it be said I walked away from my mistakes. If I've fathered a child, I'm prepared to face the consequences."

Those had been his exact words, but the way he'd looked had suggested he'd prefer to face the executioner's block. Nervously, she'd asked, "What do you mean?"

A bleak smile had touched his mouth. "Exactly what you're hoping I mean, my dear," he'd replied. "I'm not waiting for your father to come after me with a shotgun before I do the decent thing. We'll get married as soon as it can be arranged, and if anyone questions the unseemly haste of the arrangement, you can tell them in all honesty that I have to be back in Canada before the end of the month. That way you'll be safely out of sight before you start to show, and no one but you and I need to know the real reason we sprinted to the altar."

"You don't have to do this, Max," she'd said, seeing how much he hated the idea.

"Of course I do, and that's exactly what you've been counting on."

"No. Marrying me was never part of your plan."

"It was part of yours, though, wasn't it?" he'd said scornfully. "The minute you clapped eyes on me, you started casting about for a way to snag me."

"No!" she'd protested, her heart breaking. "Max, I love you!"

"You don't even know me. I could have a prison record as long as your arm and six ex-wives stashed in the closet, for all you care. What matters is that I'm rich and can afford you, and while you'd have preferred it if I'd gone down on my knees and proposed in the good, old-fashioned way, when you realized it wasn't going to happen quite that easily, you decided to help matters along even if it did mean dispensing with your moral rectitude and putting your virginity on the block. Money's a powerful aphrodisiac when you don't have any, isn't it, Gabriella?"

She'd jumped up from her chair, uncaring that people were staring. "How *dare* you insult me!" she'd gasped. "I am a Siklossy and we have never sold ourselves for money!"

"Oh, sit down and stop making a fool of yourself!" he'd said bluntly. "Your family doesn't have a pot to pee in, the old family mansion's crumbling around your ears and needs an injection of cash in the worst way, so when a nice North American millionaire came along ripe for the picking, you did what you had to, to reel him in." He'd slapped a fistful of forints on the table and leaned close. "Well, congratulations, Gabriella! I hope like hell you find it's worth what it's going to cost you."

It had not been, not for the longest time. The six months following had been the most miserable of her life. She'd often wondered if, in fact, there really had been a baby and the sheer stress surrounding the days following their farce of a wedding had caused her to miscarry, even though the specialist Max dragged her to see when the bleeding began determined otherwise.

"Your pregnancy test's negative, and there's no other physical evidence to indicate spontaneous abortion," he'd said. "Given that your cycle is irregular anyway and you've gone this long before without menstruating, it's my guess your doctor made a misdiagnosis in the first place. How soon after your last period did you see him?"

"I...didn't," she'd admitted. "I just assumed...because my husband and I had made love..."

How pathetic her reasoning had sounded; how pitifully inadequate. And yet, it had been the truth, even though she'd never convinced Max of that.

"Irregular cycle?" he'd sneered with blistering anger, afterward. "Missed periods? And it never once occurred to you to mention that small detail to me? You just let me infer you'd seen a doctor and hoped I'd never find out differently? Gee, Gabriella, you're just full of surprises, aren't you? What's next on your devious agenda? Twins left in a basket on the doorstep?"

Small wonder their marriage had turned into such a nightmare. But they'd been handed the chance to turn things around and this time, she wasn't battling on her own. She had Max on her side, and she wouldn't allow anyone or anything to drive them apart.

"Good grief!" Willow McHenry exclaimed, swanning into the room and taking a good, long look at the wedding picture. "Better put that away, Mrs. Logan, before the interviewer sees it and decides there's something, after all, to the rumor that your marriage is in trouble! Poor Max looks as if he's headed for the hangman's noose!" She traced a fingernail polished with clear enamel over his face, then flicked her gaze to his bride. "You look gorgeous though. Positively radiant. Maybe he was just nervous, wondering how he'd ever manage to live up to your expectations."

"Oh, he manages that very well," Gabriella assured her blandly. "In every possible respect. I couldn't ask for a more devoted or attentive husband."

"Really?" Willow bathed her in one of her warmest smiles and patted her arm. "Isn't it nice that you think so!"

# CHAPTER SEVEN

GABRIELLA refused to let the remark throw her off stride—even though she was quite convinced that was its primary aim. Willow worked hard to give the impression she was as warm and fuzzy as a doting mother cat, but she knew how to unsheathe her claws and though her attacks were swift and subtle, the scratches she left behind stung.

"Well, it can stay where it is, if you insist," she said, taking the photo from Gabriella and giving the glass a quick polish with the hem of the little apron she'd tied around her waist. The same apron, Gabriella realized with a small sense of shock, which she'd come across, her first day back at the penthouse.

Against her better judgment, she said, "Where did you find that apron, Willow?"

"Right where I left it, dear. In a drawer in the kitchen."

That *did* rock Gabriella's composure! Fortunately, the television crew showed up just then, and the ensuing chaos as they moved furniture, strung cables across the floor, and set lights and cameras in place, distracted her enough that she had no choice but to wait for a more appropriate time to analyze this latest affront to her peace of mind.

Whipping off the little Susie-homemaker apron, Willow donned her suit jacket again and, armed with her clipboard and pencil, reverted to self-assured executive assistant very much on the job. "I'm afraid that's out of the question," she ordained, when the interviewer, Jaclyn, a nice

woman in her early forties, suggested they might take a
few shots of the penthouse as a lead-in to the main event.
"My employer is a very private man and his home is off
limits, except for this room and possibly the south-facing
terrace. There's nothing else to see on the main floor anyway, except for the dining room and his office, and nothing but two en suite bedrooms upstairs. Nothing out of
the ordinary at all."

"Well, I find this room quite *extra*ordinary," Jaclyn
said, smiling at Gabriella and indicating the two armchairs
positioned before the cameras. "You have wonderful
taste, Mrs. Logan, and it's reflected in your choice of decor as much as in the clothes you wear so well."

"Actually, Mr. Logan chose the furnishings in here,"
Willow supplied helpfully.

"Really?" Dismissing her rather sharply, Jaclyn turned
back to Gabriella. "Let's get started, shall we?"

She began straightforwardly enough but though her
tone remained sympathetic, inevitably the subject came
around to the rumors of a troubled marriage. "You and
your husband are apart much of the time," she said tact-
fully. "How do you respond to the speculation that this
has put a severe strain on your relationship?"

"It's true that our careers often take us in different
directions, but we both recognize it's the *quality* of the
time we spend together that counts, and not necessarily
the *quantity*." Fully aware of Willow hovering in the
background, Gabriella stroked her finger fondly over the
wedding photo on the table beside her, then looked directly into the camera. "But I can say without reservation
that my husband and I have never been closer. Regardless
of what the tabloids might hint at, we have *never* been
happier."

Jaclyn leaned forward in her chair. "I find that quite

remarkable. So often, when a woman achieves the kind of success you've realized, home and family tend to fall by the wayside.''

"Not in my case," Gabriella replied emphatically. "I am even more deeply committed to my husband now than I was on the day I married him. Realistically, my career as a model will last, at most, another few years. I intend to make my marriage last a lifetime.''

She punctuated the last remark with a glance at Willow, and only her professional training kept Gabriella from recoiling at the fleeting expression she surprised on the other woman's face. The full and smiling mouth was pinched in a grimace as if its owner was hard-pressed to keep it silent, but most shocking was the unbridled rage blazing from those hitherto friendly brown eyes.

Then, just as swiftly, the genial mask fell into place again and the moment passed. "Congratulations, everybody! I think that went very well," Willow announced, resuming charge as the interview came to an end. "Gabriella, thank you for allowing us to make such a mess of your living room, but rest assured I'll see to it that everything's returned to its proper place before I leave.''

Gabriella, though, felt anything but reassured. In her line of work, she'd come across too many women eaten up with jealousy not to recognize it when it was staring her in the face. Willow might like to give the impression she was content to be known only as Ms. McHenry, Max's loyal assistant, but in reality she aspired to much more. Her ultimate goal was to be Mrs. Max Logan, and she wasn't going to let the small matter of a current wife stand in her way. And that, without question, made her Gabriella's enemy!

\* \* \*

Something was wrong. He heard it in Gabriella's voice when he phoned to tell her he wouldn't make it back before Wednesday afternoon, after all, and he heard it again when he called from Denver to explain his connecting flight was delayed because of mechanical problems. Her responses were too careful. Too flat. And that made him uneasy as hell, though if truth be told he'd been antsy ever since the previous week's unsettling conversation with Willow.

He'd thought they understood each other; had believed she recognized that incident eight months earlier for what it really had been: the brief and isolated lapse in judgment of a lonely man who came to his senses before any real damage had been done.

Now, he was no longer so sure Willow saw things quite that way. His gut instinct warned him that what he'd long ago dismissed as something that ended before it properly began, she had blown out of all proportion and turned into a major affair. He couldn't put his finger on anything specific; it was more that a lot of little things, though piddling in themselves, assumed disturbing significance when added together.

He wasn't a superstitious man, and he didn't believe in courting trouble. But he was no fool either. He knew better than anyone that if it did occur, ignoring it wouldn't make it disappear. A man who wanted to stay in control of his own life and protect the people and things he cared about, had to take action and neutralize a problem *before* it ran amok.

He and Gabriella had come a long way in the last week, and he wasn't about to stand idly by and watch their marriage go down the tubes through any default on his part. Perhaps he needed to be more proactive in making that crystal clear to the world in general—and to Willow in particular. Conveniently, the next night's awards dinner would provide him with the ideal opportunity to do precisely that.

He hoped she'd be smart enough to get the message, but if she chose to be obtuse, he was perfectly prepared to spell it out for her, one syllable at a time. And if *that* wasn't enough to convince her she was pinning the tail on the wrong donkey, he'd fire her and to hell with the possible repercussions. He wasn't about to be held up to ransom by her, or anyone else.

It was close to midnight when he finally arrived at his own front door. The penthouse was silent and only one lamp in the foyer had been left on. Gabriella was half asleep, and although he'd have liked nothing more than to make love to her, he was pretty bushed himself. So, foregoing the pleasure until they were both in better shape to appreciate it, he crawled into bed, wrapped his arms around her, and fell into the deep and dreamless sleep of a man confident that he had a firm hold on more than just his wife's warm, delicious, sweetly scented body.

When she stepped into the reception area outside the hotel's vast mirrored ballroom on Thursday night, Gabriella decided she could just as well have been attending an opening at one of the world's most recognized fashion houses. Certainly, every designer she'd ever worked with was represented in the gorgeous silks and beaded creations worn by the women around her.

And the jewels! Diamonds that put the fire of the crystal chandeliers to shame; Colombian emeralds, pigeon's blood rubies, sapphires the size of walnuts! Absently, she fingered the aquamarine lying snugly at her throat.

Noticing, Max murmured, "It might not be the showiest piece in the room, but it's hanging around the most beautiful neck.''

She loved the way he leaned into her when he spoke, the movement so slight as to go unnoticed by a casual observer, but possessed of such a subtle intimacy that a tiny explosion of delight vibrated throughout her body. She loved the way he looked, too. There wasn't a man in the room who matched his black-tie elegance.

''It's perfect and I wouldn't change it for the world,'' she said.

His gaze slid to the Swarowski crystal studs in her ears. ''I should have commissioned matching earrings.''

''You had my wedding ring resized so that I can wear it again.'' She brushed a minuscule thread of lint from the satin lapel of his dinner jacket, and let her left hand drift up to caress his jaw, loving the way the light gleamed on the simple gold band as she did so. He'd given it to her after she'd finished dressing that evening, and as he'd slipped it on her finger, she'd promised herself she'd never take it off again, no matter what. ''This means more to me than any number of expensive gifts.''

''Unless you want to cause a scene, quit touching me like that,'' he growled, snagging her wrist. ''It's been almost four days since we made love and I'm feeling deprived.''

''Me, too,'' she told him on a shaken breath, the heat he so easily aroused with a glance, a word, streaking through her. ''I missed you so much when you were away, Max.''

She wanted to tell him she loved him, too, but not until after he'd said it to her. Only then could she be sure he was ready to hear the words he'd steadfastly refused to believe when she'd spoken them to him in the past.

He raised her hand. Kissed the pulse beating at her

inner wrist. Traced a covert, sensual circle in her palm with his thumb, and nodded to where her parents were engaged in animated conversation with the Austrian consul and his wife. "What do you say to us making up for lost time by cutting out of here early? We can send the limo back to collect your folks later."

"I hope I didn't just hear what I thought I heard!" Willow McHenry, demurely resplendent in bronze taffeta, materialized out of the crowd, champagne glass in hand. "You can't possibly leave early, Max. It's out of the question."

*Out of the question,* Gabriella thought with some amusement, tripped off Willow's tongue with practiced ease any time events threatened to disrupt her well-orchestrated plans. Hopefully, she'd soon apply it to her secret hopes for a more intimate liaison with Max!

During his absence, Gabriella had had plenty of time to mull over Tuesday's events and remained more convinced than ever that her instincts were on target. Even her mother had commented on the proprietary way Willow had taken over. "She thinks I am too old and unimportant to be of any consequence," Maria had said darkly, "but I am still smart enough to recognize a snake when it slithers into my daughter's home. Beware of her, my child. She is dangerous."

The snake had wound itself around Max's other arm. The brief glance he spared it, and the speed with which he disentangled himself made Gabriella glad she'd decided not to undermine their reconciliation by voicing her suspicions to him. He'd said "it"—whatever *it* had been—was over, and if she couldn't take his word over Willow McHenry's, she had no business wearing his ring and passing herself off as his wife now.

"There must be five hundred people here, Willow," he said tersely. "I doubt we'd be missed."

"Of course you'd be missed!" She swung her gaze to include Gabriella and bared her teeth in a smile. "Both of you. It's not often the city scene's brightened by a celebrity of your wife's magnitude, on top of which tonight my boss is a star in his own right, as well." Undeterred by the way he'd shrugged her off, she tucked her hand beneath his elbow and nodded toward the waiters setting plates of smoked salmon on the linen-draped tables in the ballroom. "I think we should find our seats, don't you? It looks as if dinner's about to be served."

*Your wife…my boss?* Amazing!

Biting her lips to stifle the giggle threatening to erupt, Gabriella marveled at how, one way or another, the woman managed to worm her way into their private universe and turn them from a couple to a trio. "Are you here alone, Willow?" she inquired politely, when she managed to bring herself under control again.

Willow's gaze narrowed, but her smiled gleamed as implacably as ever. "Of course not, dear. Here's my date now. Max, you already know Brent, I believe?"

Max shook the man's hand. "Sure. Nice to see you here, Brent."

"And this," Willow continued with superbly subtle contempt, "is the famous Gabriella Siklossy, Brent."

"Also known as my wife," Max put in blandly, placing a possessive hand at Gabriella's waist and inching her a little closer. "Brent works in the drafting department at Logan Enterprises, sweetheart, and drew up some of the preliminary plans for the Budapest project."

The three of them chatted briefly about the success of the restoration and the charm of her native city in general, and for once Willow was unable to insinuate herself into the conversation.

That she didn't like being relegated to the sidelines was obvious. "It's never been on my travel agenda," she said brusquely when, in an attempt to include her, Gabriella asked if she'd visited eastern Europe.

She immediately reasserted herself, though, when they reached their table. "I think you should sit here, next to the podium, Max," she proclaimed. "That way, you won't have to climb over our laps to get to the microphone."

The little laugh she tacked on to her remark was meant to imply she was joking, of course, but Gabriella was willing to bet Willow would give up six months' salary for the chance to get better acquainted with Max's lap— or any other part of him she could lay hands on. In all honesty, Gabriella could hardly blame her. He was the most gorgeous man in the room, and quite possibly the entire world!

Her tolerance was short-lived though, when the relentless woman tried to relegate her to a seat about as far removed from Max's as it was possible to get, short of moving her to another table. "And you over here, with your mother and father, Gabriella."

Once again, Max intervened. "My wife, her parents, and I will sit together, Willow."

"Oh…!" She shrugged indifferently. "All right, if you say so. But I was rather hoping you'd give the rest of us a chance to rub shoulders with your famous guests. Sort of share in the reflected glory, if you see what I mean."

"Afraid you'll have to make do with admiring them from a distance," he said, his voice cut with steel. "And just for the record, I don't share my wife with anyone."

Although warmed by his words, a thread of uneasiness

wove through Gabriella. Was it her imagination, or was he playing the attentive husband with a little too much dedication tonight? And if so, for whose benefit?

"I don't mind mingling," she told him.

He ushered her to her chair and took a seat next to her. "I do," he said. "I want you by my side, close enough to touch."

She had never felt more secure, never more certain that they belonged together. If only they could have done as he'd suggested and slipped away when the meal was over, how differently the evening might have ended. But a person's whole world could come crashing down on *if only's,* and Gabriella's began to fall apart in the lull between dessert and the presentation of awards.

She had slipped away to the ladies' room and was seated on a stool at the vanity table, touching up her lipstick, when the door opened and Willow came in. Their eyes met in the mirror and although there was a steady stream of traffic in and out, an irrational sense of danger swept over Gabriella, raising the hair on the back of her neck and sending tiny thrills of fear chasing over her skin.

"I thought I might find you in here." All cozy smiles, Willow plopped onto the stool next to hers. "I've been waiting all night to tell you how perfectly divine you look, and I absolutely adore your pendant." As if they were very old, very good friends, she leaned across and scooped the aquamarine onto the pad of her finger in order to examine it more closely. "It's one of Gio's pieces, of course. The craftsmanship and design are unmistakable. Was it a gift from Max?"

"Yes," Gabriella said, trying not to shrink at the touch of that cool, intrusive finger at her throat.

"Well, aren't you lucky! All he ever gave me from there are these." She let go of the pendant, and tilted her head to show off the topaz-and-gold studs in her ears. "Not that I'm complaining, mind you, since the most expensive thing I've ever given him is the pen set he keeps on his desk at the office—oh, no, that's not quite true!" She tapped a reproving forefinger against her pursed lips. "I gave him the marble clock beside his bed, too. But that hardly counts, because it was my fault the one he had before got broken."

Apparently oblivious to the impact of that little gem of information, she turned to the mirror and pushed her fingers through her hair, arranging a curl here, another there, then leaning forward to inspect her teeth, presumably to make sure no debris from the spinach soufflé accompanying the main course had overstayed its welcome.

"How could it have been your fault?" If it hadn't been that she suddenly found herself floundering like a nonswimmer tossed into a bottomless lake, Gabriella would have rejoiced at how unperturbed she managed to sound.

"Hmm?" Another curl was lovingly tucked into place. "Oh, you mean about the clock? I knocked it off the bedside table by accident, one night. I suppose I could have had it repaired, but things like that generally aren't worth what it costs to have them fixed, and it was rather badly smashed, so I decided to buy him a new one instead."

"Not worth fixing? For your information, it had a one-of-a-kind crystal case signed by the artist and—"

"Tell me about it! I was afraid to walk barefoot on the carpet for days afterward."

*Don't assume the worst!* Gabriella told herself sternly. *Just because she's been in your bedroom doesn't necessarily mean she's been in your bed as well! She's playing some sort of sick mind game and if you want to emerge the winner, you'll walk away from her. Now! Only a devil for punishment would leave herself open to further injury by asking her what she was doing upstairs in your home to begin with.*

So true! But sometimes, the only way to put an end to the doubts was to drag them out into the clear light of day and confront them. How else to lay them to rest and go forward with one's life? No matter what the outcome, anything was preferable to leaving them to fester like some insidious disease.

Replacing the cap on her lipstick, she took a tissue from the box on the vanity table and blotted her lips. "What were you doing in our bedroom, Willow?" she asked, proud of the cool detachment in her voice. She was the only one who knew she was shaking inside. With fear, with pain, with anger.

A smile so slight it was almost a smirk crossed Willow's face. "Among other things, I was sleeping in there, dear."

*Among other things? The witch!* "With Max's permission?"

Willow glanced at her, eyebrows raised in astonishment. "Don't look so shocked, Gabriella. Certainly with Max's permission! What did you think? That I just wandered in there uninvited and made myself at home?" She sighed, and a faraway look came into her eyes before she let them drift closed. "That mattress was pure heaven, just as Max promised!"

Perhaps if she hadn't been blindsided by shock, Gabriella might have managed to handle the situation with more poise. She was, after all, a woman of the world, and men cheating on their wives was hardly a novel concept. Some might even go so far as to say that, in Max's case, it was justified; that she'd driven him to it by walking out on him and leaving him to his own devices too long. She might even have believed it herself and been able to forgive him—*if he hadn't sworn to her that he'd remained faithful.*

It was this last betrayal of trust that unraveled her and had her leaping up from the stool so violently that it tipped over. She didn't care that two other women who'd been chatting together on a love seat in the corner eyed her suspiciously and practically tripped over each other in their eagerness to leave before the catfight began. "You're lying! You've never set foot in my bedroom!"

Oh, how shrill she sounded. How pathetically hysterical.

"I'm afraid I have, dear," Willow said, calmly collecting her bag and standing up also. "And in your lovely luxurious soaker tub, too. My stars, it's almost as comfortable as the mattress and vastly preferable to the shower! And I'll never forget the view from the bed on a clear night. There's nothing quite like being all warm and cozy under the covers and watching the moon rise over the sea, don't you agree?"

Gabriella simply stared at her, too speechless with dismay to muster a reply. Instead, she stood frozen with incredulity as Willow patted her cheek and admonished kindly, "Pull yourself together, dear. It's high time we got back to our table and you don't want some photographer capturing you looking like this and splashing your picture all over tomorrow morning's paper, now do you?"

That soft little hand, the phony, concerned smile, the anxious query in the brown eyes which weren't anxious at all, but completely empty and without soul—the combination was more than Gabriella could bear. *"Don't touch me!"* she whispered, springing back with a shudder. *"Don't ever come near me again."*

"Well, if you prefer to spend the rest of the night sulking in here, that's your business." Willow shrugged. "But don't worry, I'm certainly not going to insist on staying with you and holding your hand through yet another emotional crisis. No wonder poor Max got tired of trying to keep you happy. I can see now why he felt he was wasting his time.''

She swept out and let the door swish closed behind her. Alone in the blessed silence, Gabriella set the stool upright again and collapsed on its padded seat. *So, finally, the gloves were off!*

She supposed she ought to be relieved. But she felt nothing. Was so numb, in fact, that she wondered briefly if she was trapped in some horrible dream brought on by too much champagne. Except she'd drunk barely two glasses all night, and the tears glazing her cheeks were hot and wet and all too real.

A few minutes later, the door swung open again. Too distraught to face anyone, Gabriella fled around the corner and into the nearest toilet stall. Footsteps followed and stopped on the other side of the cool marble wall behind which she hid. ''Gabriella,'' her mother said softly. ''I've come to help.''

It was perhaps the one voice in the entire world capable of melting the ice encasing her heart; the only voice that had always known how to heal the hurts. And oh, how she was hurting, now that the numbness was wearing off! So much so that her face was contorted with the pain, and great ugly noises were coming from her mouth.

''Open the door, my darling,'' her mother coaxed.

And she did. Because her mother would love her no matter how she looked or sounded. She didn't have to pretend to be brave or impervious or invincible, and she didn't have to be perfect. All she'd ever had to do for her mother to love her was be herself.

''Oh, Mama!'' she wept, sliding back the bolt and falling into her mother's arms. ''I think I'm going to die!''

''Rubbish!'' her mother said. ''You have too much to

live for. Wash your face, then come and sit on that little couch where all the mirrors are, and tell me what's gone so terribly wrong in the last half hour that you're hiding in here like a refugee. Your poor husband's beside himself with worry. I believe if I hadn't come myself to investigate, he *would* have.''

Oh, how tempted she was to unburden herself! How she wished she could paint a truthful picture of her troubled marriage and solicit her mother's advice, lean on her wisdom! Yet what right had she to weigh down a seventy-year-old woman with such knowledge, then expect her to return with an easy mind to a home on the other side of the world?

No, her mother deserved better. Both her parents did. It was for their sake that she'd entered into the charade of happy wife in the first place, and she did not have the right to shatter the image now. With only two more days left in their holiday, she had an obligation to preserve the myth, no matter how painful or difficult she might find it.

Clamping her fingers to her mouth to stop its trembling, she took a deep breath. ''You're right, Mama,'' she admitted shakily. ''Sometimes, I say the first thing that comes into my head without any thought for whether or not it makes sense. Of course I'm not dying. But for a little while, it felt as if I might.''

''Did that woman say or do something to upset you, darling? She's the one who told me I ought to come looking for you.''

Gabriella forced a smile to her lips and shook her head. ''It was something I ate. Suddenly, I felt...'' The memory of Willow's self-satisfied smirk rose up in her mind, and a tremor of distaste ran over her, revolting as insect feet. ''...very unwell. But I'm better now.''

Her mother watched her a moment, her eyes so full of love and compassion that Gabriella's heart broke all over again. "Yes," she said. "I think you are. Or if not, then you will be. Comb your pretty hair, my darling, and pinch your cheeks to make them rosy again. Max has won a prestigious award for his work preserving old buildings, and you should be at his side helping him celebrate his success."

She could not face him again, not tonight, not after what she'd learned. And yet, if she did not, wouldn't she just be playing into Willow McHenry's merciless little hands?

"I will," she said. "I just need a moment to myself. Go back to the table, Mama, and tell him I'll be there soon."

She waited until she was alone before daring to look in the mirror again. She was not a pretty sight. Her face was blotchy, her eyes red-rimmed. As for her famous smile, she doubted she'd ever be able to produce it again. If he could see her now, her agent would probably ask to be released from his contract, certain her career was over.

But she hadn't climbed to the top of her profession without learning a few tricks on the way. Cold water was a model's best friend; never being caught without basic essentials the one unbreakable law which ruled her life. A little concealer under the eyes, a touch of pressed powder to nose and cheeks, a stroke of mascara on the lashes, and long, soothing sweeps of the miniature hair brush she'd tucked in her bag, worked a minor miracle. Add a spine of steel, and the makeover was complete.

Smoothing the long full skirt of her dress over her hips, she stepped back and flung a last challenging glance at her image. "Curtain time, Gabriella," she announced softly, then, head held high, she turned to the door and prepared to face her nemesis.

## CHAPTER EIGHT

SHE found Max impatiently pacing the hallway outside. "What the devil took you so long, sweetheart? I was beginning to think you'd moved in there permanently."

"Don't think I wasn't tempted," she shot back, ignoring his proffered hand and sailing past him under her own steam into the ballroom.

The shimmering light from the chandeliers had been dimmed so that only the glow of candles was reflected in the mirrored walls, and those people who weren't chatting over after-dinner drinks were dancing to a small orchestra. But what should have been a dream setting had turned into a nightmare for Gabriella.

Max caught up with her before she'd taken more than half a dozen steps. "Ahem! Want to talk about whatever's got you so steamed?"

"Not right at this moment, no." She smiled and nodded at the Austrian consul and his wife as they pirouetted past. "Congratulations, by the way. I hear you won an award."

"Screw the award, Gabriella!" Max snapped, grabbing her by the arm and swinging her around to face him just as she was about to plunge through the crowd to their table. "And while you're at it, screw the frozen attitude, too! Something's up and I want to know what it is."

She steeled herself to meet his gaze. Until that night, she'd never been able to look into his candid blue eyes without her heart doing a little flip-flop somersault. But that was before she'd been given reason to suspect he was, above all else, a consummate liar. Now, she was afraid she'd either slap his face or burst into tears.

"This is neither the time nor the place, Max. It can wait."

He flung an exasperated glare at the people swirling past them. "Fine. If you won't talk, we'll dance. Because I'm damned if you're going to treat me as if I'm not even here!"

"I don't want to dance with you."

"Prove it." He pulled her against him, locked one arm around her waist, and positioned his hand in the small of her back with sufficient pressure to mold her hips to his. Disguised by the folds of her skirt, he forced his knee between both of hers, leaving her with the choice of moving with him as he began a sultry waltz, or remaining stationary and having him rub up against her in a way that was downright indecent.

"I am not enjoying this," she informed him starchily.

"Oh, yes, you are," he said, bringing their joined hands to rest against his chest, and brushing his knuckles over her breasts until she thought her nipples would self-destruct. "I've got you so hot and bothered, you can barely stand up."

He wasn't always a liar. Sometimes, he homed in on the truth all too well. If she didn't sit down soon, she'd fall down. Her legs were trembling and the ache between her thighs had left her moist with heated longing. "Don't be ridiculous!" she said.

He laughed and nuzzled his mouth to her ear. And what he was doing with his hips didn't bear thinking about! "You forget how well I know your beautiful body, my love. I recognize what it's telling me."

"You're the one with the erection, not me," she said boldly. "You should be ashamed of yourself."

"Why? Because I find dancing with my wife such a turn-on?"

"I wish they'd turn on the overhead lights," she fumed. "I bet you wouldn't be quite so cocky then!"

For once, she actually managed to leave him at a loss for words. He stopped dead in the middle of the floor, his arms fell to his sides, and if it weren't that she was so hurt and bewildered by the confrontation with Willow, she'd have laughed at the conflicting expressions chasing over his face.

He recovered quickly though, and bathed her in a smile so dazzling and engaging, it tore holes in her already battered heart. "Was that a deliberate double entendre, or merely your way of showing off how well versed you've become in colloquialisms?"

A furious blush engulfed her then, as the import of what she'd said sank home. "Trust you to put the worst possible connotation on every little word that comes out of my mouth! But then, what else should I expect from a man with the morals of a goat!"

Her eyes were brimming with tears, and she didn't care who saw them. He did, though. "Hey," he said, drawing her back into his arms. "What have morals got to do with anything? You know I'm just teasing you, so what's really going on here, Gabriella?"

He wore such a look of concern, invested such a wealth of tenderness in his question, that she was sorely tempted to lean into his embrace and spill out everything bottled up inside her. But just then the music stopped and before she could speak, another voice intruded—one she'd come to despise for the venom underlying the syrup that coated every word.

"Oh, *there* you are, dear!" Willow crooned, feigning solicitude. "I was just on my way back to the ladies' room to find out if you were feeling better, but I can see I was worrying needlessly.''

*''What's going on?''* Gabriella glared at Max. ''Why don't you ask *her?* She's the one with all the answers.''

He stepped back a pace and looked from her to Willow, his eyes very cagey all of a sudden, but his face otherwise wiped clean of all expression. ''Because I'm asking you, and I'm getting tired of waiting for an answer that makes sense.''

''I'm afraid,'' she said, tossing her head contemptuously, ''that what I have to say isn't something you really want to hear.''

''Gabriella, stop this!''

Once upon a time, she'd have heeded that imperious command. She'd have walked through fire, if he'd ordered her to do so. But those days were over. Ignoring him, she plowed through the crush of bodies to the double doors that opened onto the curving balcony overlooking the main lobby of the hotel, and down the escalator to the back entrance where a doorman was hailing taxis for departing guests.

The evening had long ago lost whatever charm it might once have held for her, and all she wanted now was for it to be over.

''Let her go, Max.'' Willow grabbed a pit bull hold on his arm when he tried to follow Gabriella. ''There's nothing you can do.''

''The hell there isn't!'' he snapped, shaking her off. ''What have you said to my wife, that she looks ready to take a chain saw to both of us?''

''Nothing.'' She gazed at him, all wide-eyed innocence. ''Nothing but the truth.''

He stopped dead in his tracks at that, knowing with

sinking certainty that it had been a truth custom-designed to suit Willow's purposes and undermine all his efforts to shore up his sagging marriage. A cold sweat prickled unpleasantly over his skin. "Whose truth, Willow?" he inquired, closing in on her menacingly. "Yours?"

"Really, Max!" She raised her hands and placed both palms flat against his chest. "You're making a scene. Calm down!"

"I'm not in the mood to calm down. I'm going after my wife, and when I find her, I'm..."

*Going to wring her neck! Then I'm coming back to wring yours!*

Choking back the threat, he pushed past her and cut a swath through the packed room, following the direction Gabriella had taken. Leaning over the low glass wall of the mezzanine, he scanned the area below, searching for a glimpse of her and spotted her almost immediately. With her looks and in that eye-catching dress, she was hard to miss.

She stood at the concierge's desk, scribbling something on a piece of paper. Not ten yards away, revolving glass doors opened onto the porticoed parking area where a fleet of limos and taxis waited. Another minute, and she'd be gone.

Luckily, the mezzanine was relatively deserted. He made it down the escalator in record time and practically sprinted across the main lobby, coming up behind her just as she handed the note to the concierge.

"Please have this message delivered to Mr. and Mrs. Zoltan Siklossy at table six in the Crystal Ballroom," she instructed him.

"That won't be necessary," Max said, intercepting the folded slip of paper and crumpling it into a ball.

At the sound of his voice, she swung around, practically

spitting with fury. Looked so much like an exotic cat about to attack, in fact, that if he hadn't been so royally ticked off himself, he'd have applauded. Her huge aquamarine eyes had narrowed to slits, her teeth were bared in a grimace, her silky blond hair flew around her head like a mane.

And still she managed to look stupendous. Tall and proud and aristocratic, with the bottle-green satin of her strapless dress glowing against her honey-gold skin and swirling rich and full around her long, magnificent legs.

Then she spoke, bursting into wild, impassioned Hungarian, which was just as well because he didn't need an interpreter to tell him that she'd probably have been arrested if she'd resorted to English.

"Settle down," he ordered.

He'd have been better off keeping his mouth shut and exercising muscle instead, because all he succeeded in doing was stoking her rage to greater heights. Talk about putting on a show! Her performance held the concierge and two bellhops paralyzed with fascination.

Well, they might be enjoying it, but he'd had his fill of melodrama for one night. "Gabriella!" he thundered.

Her mouth remained open but the torrent of noise stopped. Knowing it was a temporary cease-fire only, he wasted no time on persuasion or diplomacy.

"We will take this some place private," he informed her. "You might not care that you're making a fool of yourself, but I do."

"I refuse to remain here with the two of you!"

*Two?* He'd have thought she was hallucinating on top of everything else if a quick glance over his shoulder hadn't revealed Willow bringing up the rear. *Just peachy!*

Dismissing her with a glare, he turned back to his wife. "You'll damn well do as you're told, for once," he advised her. Then, fishing a fifty-dollar bill out of his wallet, he snapped his fingers to bring the concierge out of his trance. "Find us a room where we can be alone."

"At once, sir." Palming the tip, the man hustled them into the small office behind his desk. Lit by a single bulb and equipped only with a wooden table, a couple of chairs and a spare coatrack, it hardly matched the elegance of the public rooms, but it served the purpose.

"Okay." Fists on his hips, Max eyeballed his wife. "Start talking, Gabriella, before I really lose patience."

"And make sure you stick to the facts!"

He whirled around, realizing too late that Willow had followed them into the office. "I don't recall inviting you to join the party."

The way she leaned against the door made it clear the only way she was leaving was if he threw her out bodily. "I have the right to defend myself against this woman's insane accusations."

Gabriella let out a hiss and lunged forward. She was taller than Willow by a good five inches, and though there wasn't much meat on her bones, what she did have was toned to perfection. Willow would end up picking her teeth out of the carpet if it came to a wrestling match and loath though he was to defend her, Max felt obligated to intervene on her behalf.

"Gabriella, for crying out loud!" Not sure of the protocol for breaking up a catfight, he grabbed her around the waist and swung her off her feet.

Her high heel caught him a sharp blow on the shin, one flailing fist connected with his jaw, an elbow jabbed him in the ribs. And as if that wasn't punishment enough, she let fly with another Hungarian tongue-lashing.

Alarmed, Willow shrank against the door and he couldn't say he blamed her. Given a choice, he'd opt for a football scrimmage any day of the week over trying to contain a woman on the warpath! "Listen, Gabriella," he panted in her ear, pinning her arms and hauling her against him so that her shoulders were sandwiched to his chest, "keep this up, and someone's going to get hurt. I'd as soon avoid that, and if you stop to think about it, I think you'll agree with me."

"Precisely," Willow chimed in. "Lay a hand on me, Gabriella Siklossy, and I'll slap you with assault charges so fast, you won't know what hit you. Just think what *that*'ll do for your public image!"

*"Peasant!"* Gabriella spat.

"Put a lid on it, both of you, and start acting your age!" he bellowed. "I've had it up to here with your histrionics! I don't know what the devil's gone down between the two of you tonight, and I'm beginning not to care."

Wrong thing to say! Gabriella wriggled around and tried her damnedest to knee him in his most delicate parts. "You've never cared!" she cried. "You announce at dinner that you don't share your wife, but you expect her to share you! If I weren't here now, you'd probably throw that…that *creature* down on the table and have sex with her. But then, it wouldn't be nearly as comfortable or private as our bed, would it, and she couldn't wash the smell of you off her body in our bathtub afterward, could she?"

"You want to tell me what the hell she's talking about?" he asked Willow.

Apparently not sure he had the situation fully under control, she pushed away from the door but kept a wary eye on Gabriella. "It's really very simple. I ran into your wife in the ladies' room. We compared jewelry and in the course of making pleasant conversation, I happened to mention how much I'd enjoyed living in the penthouse.

She became totally unhinged and went so far as to call me a liar in front of an audience. I'd appreciate it if you'd set her straight on the matter.''

"Gabriella?" He relaxed his hold slightly. "Is that all there was to it?"

"It's not *enough?*" she exclaimed, vibrating with outrage. "First, you buy her expensive earrings, then you move her into my home?"

"No, it's not quite enough," he said, "but it'll do for now."

"You don't *deny* it?"

"No," he said. "Basically, she told you the truth. Too bad it never occurred to you there might be more to the story."

She squirmed to face him. "Then defend yourself! Show me that I can trust your word over hers!"

"Why? What difference would it make? You've already judged me and found me guilty."

"Max, *please!*" The anger was seeping out of her like water running down a drain. But instead of feeling vindicated, he knew only a sense of defeat. Of resignation.

"You see?" Willow said smugly, reading his expression. "There's absolutely no pleasing her, no matter how hard you try."

"And what would it take to please you, Willow?" he asked.

"Well, an apology from her, for a start."

"I'll see that you get it."

"Never!" Gabriella exclaimed haughtily. "I will not apologize to the woman who has done her best to steal my husband."

He pushed her down on one of the chairs and leaned over her. "Yes, Gabriella, you *will* apologize because, strictly speaking, every word she told you is the truth.

And when you have, I'll fill in all the important little bits she somehow forgot to mention, and you'll see you have no reason to believe I've ever betrayed you. Perhaps then, you'll feel like apologizing to me, too.''

"Max…!" Her hands fluttered helplessly, then fell into her lap. She stared up at him, her lovely eyes wide with distress. "If I've misunderstood, please tell me how!"

"The apology comes first, Gabriella."

She drew in a long, deep breath and for a moment he thought her pride might get in the way and she'd tell them both to go to hell. Then she slowly rose to her feet, straightened her impeccable spine, and pinned Willow in that compelling green gaze. "I'm sorry if I have accused you unjustly, and I apologize."

Just that. No beating around the bush with excuses, just a straightforward admission uttered with all the dignity and grace of a true aristocrat. He hoped he could carry through with what he had to say, with half her class.

"Okay," he began. "First, the earrings were in recognition of the extra hours Willow put in to help save a project that would have gone down the tubes otherwise. Instead, it paid off handsomely, and I acknowledged my gratitude in similar ways to everyone on my staff who gave up evenings and weekends to get the job done. The women got earrings, the men watches."

"Well, if I'd known that, I'd—"

"Second, she had to vacate her leaky condo for a month while it was being repaired, so I offered her the use of the penthouse. If it matters at all, I happened to be in Cairo the entire time she stayed."

Gabriella moistened her lips with the tip of her tongue. "I see."

"Yes," he said wearily, "I'm sure you do, now. The

pity of it is, you didn't see fit to come to me for the answers in the first place.''

''How was I to know there was more to her story?''

''Because you know me, Gabriella. At least, I thought you did. And I thought we'd agreed we'd be up front with each other about any concerns or questions we might have. Apparently, I was wrong on both counts.''

He turned again to Willow. ''Is there anything else I can do for you?''

''No, Max. All is forgiven.''

''Not quite,'' he said. ''I'd like your resignation on my desk first thing tomorrow.''

Aghast, she stared at him. *''Why?''*

He'd have felt sorry for her if he'd had a drop of pity left in him. But he was so choked, it was all he could do to be civil. ''Because there's a world of difference in the way we interpret the truth, Willow.''

''I won't do it,'' she said, her face pale with disbelief.

''Then I'll fire you.''

''You can't!''

''Watch me!'' he said harshly. ''Not only will I fire you, I'll sue you for sexual harassment.''

''*You*'ll sue *me*?'' She laughed. ''I think not! You seem to have forgotten about a certain night when you lured me to the penthouse and poured wine down my throat—''

''And kissed you. I haven't forgotten.''

Jeez, but he was a fool! He'd seen this coming for weeks but, in the end, done nothing to defuse it. So much for his belief in confronting trouble head-on!

''Then you might want to reconsider asking me to resign.''

''Before you think about trying to blackmail me, Willow, let me remind you that the incident to which you refer took place nearly nine months ago, that you arrived at my front door uninvited, brought the wine in question, and showed yourself more than willing to engage in an affair with me, even though you knew I was married. You even went so far as to follow up with a letter stating as much."

"You received no such letter from me!"

"No, I didn't. But you did write it, and were careless enough to leave a copy of it on your desk. And I'm perfectly prepared to produce it as evidence, if I have to."

He was bluffing, of course. He'd shredded the letter months ago. But she didn't have to know that.

"So this is what it comes down to, is it? You'll fire me to placate the woman who walked out on you and left me to pick up the pieces?"

"You leave me little choice."

He thought he knew all there was to know about her. He'd seen her at her most efficient, her most sympathetic, her most charming, and at her most vulnerable. But he'd never seen the controlled rage that crept over her features then. "This is my reward for all those times I listened while you poured your heart out about the mistakes you made with her? For the times I picked up your dry cleaning, made sure your passport was renewed on time, filled in as your hostess?"

Her voice quavered; her big brown eyes filled with tears. "I remembered your birthday. I made fruitcake for you at Christmas, and fudge. I even sewed a button on your jacket once! And not one of those things was part of my job description."

"That's not to say I didn't appreciate your efforts."

"I don't want your appreciation!" she wailed. "I want *you*, and I thought, in time, you'd see how much better off you'd be with someone like me." She pointed a distraught finger at Gabriella. "I might not be beautiful like *her,* but I'd look after you. You'd never come home to an empty house. You'd never have to go out to get a decent meal. I'd be there, whenever you needed me. I'd *never* leave you the way she did. I wouldn't steal the limelight every time we went out in public. I'd give you babies and make you proud and…''

The words dissolved into a sob.

''The only flaw in all that, Willow,'' he said gently, ''is that I never saw you in any role other than my executive assistant. I admire and respect you for what you brought to the job, but that's as far as it goes.''

The tears rolled unchecked down her cheeks. ''It could have been more, if she'd stayed away!''

''No. And that isn't going to change, regardless of where my wife chooses to live.''

''Then I guess there's nothing more to say.'' With a mighty effort, she wrenched herself under control and smeared the back of her hand across her wet cheeks.

''I'll have Brent paged and get him to take you home,'' he said, because it was the kindest way to put an end to a scene which had already dragged on too long.

''I'm sure he'll be delighted to oblige. You're the boss, after all, and what you say goes, doesn't it?'' she said sullenly. ''I suppose you want the earrings back, as well. Well, why not? You've taken away everything else I ever cared about.''

''Keep the earrings, Willow. You earned them.''

''I'd rather have earned your love.''

*Love?* The word lingered like bad wine on his palate in the silence she left behind. If lying and manipulating amounted to love, he wanted nothing to do with it.

After a moment, Gabriella came to where he slumped against the table and slipped her hand into his. ''Oh,

Max,'' she murmured, ''I feel so sorry for her! And it's all my fault! If I'd listened to you—''

Pointedly, he freed his hand and checked his watch. ''Look at that—after midnight already. The do upstairs must be winding down. Go get your parents while I line up our limo.''

He must have sounded as peeved as he felt because she looked at him anxiously. ''But you and I will talk later?''

''Enough's been said, for one night, Gabriella.''

For a lifetime, come to that. Because, as the old saying went, the more things changed, the more they stayed the same.

Impassively, he watched her leave. It was the one thing he could always count on her doing well.

Max barely said a word on the way home but her parents were very tired and seemed not to notice. They declined her offer of hot chocolate, and went straight upstairs as soon as they reached the penthouse.

Alone in the big living room, Gabriella faced her husband, tension arcing between them like invisible lightning. ''Is there anything I can get for you, Max?''

''No.'' He ripped loose his bow tie. ''Go to bed, Gabriella. If I want something, I'll get it myself.''

''You're not coming up with me?''

He looked her over from head to toe with such slow and scrupulous attention to every detail of her appearance that even she, used as she was to being in the public eye, found herself twitching nervously.

''No,'' he finally said again. ''You're a very desirable woman and despite everything that's gone down tonight, I'm not sure I trust myself not to make love to you.''

She shrugged and drummed up a smile to cover the

ominous uncertainty sweeping over her. "Would that be so very terrible?"

"It would be disastrous," he said harshly. "I'm realistic enough to recognize a lost cause when it's staring me in the face. You and I are not going to work out, Gabriella, much though we might wish we could."

His words struck a dull, thudding pain to her solar plexus. "You're giving up on us, because of what happened at the hotel?"

"Name one good reason why I shouldn't."

"I love you!" she cried, reaching for him. "Enough to fight for you, which I surely proved tonight."

"Wrong," he said. "All you proved is that when it comes down to the crunch, we play by different rules."

"We were happy until Willow came between us with her half-truths!"

He went to stand at the open doors leading to the roof garden, and took a deep breath as if to cleanse his lungs of the air she breathed. "Willow is not the problem, Gabriella," he said flatly, staring out at the bright city lights. "*We* are. The only way she was able to come between us tonight was because we let her. And the only thing we proved tonight is that our marriage is too fragile to withstand any sort of outside pressure."

"How can you say that? We won."

"That might be your idea of a victory, Gabriella, but it's not mine. I'd rather have no marriage than one so flawed that I never know from one day to the next if it's going to fall apart because of some imagined sin on my part."

She'd remained standing by the sofa, but anger sent her rushing over to grab him by the sleeve and haul him around to face her. "You listen to me, Max Logan! I'd find your holier-than-thou attitude a bit easier to swallow if you weren't every bit as much to blame as I am for the state our marriage is in. You never miss a chance to throw it in my face that I've deceived you in the past, but I notice *you*'re not above resorting to blatant lies when it suits your purpose.''

''I have never knowingly lied to you.''

He bore no resemblance at all to the man who'd seduced her with such tender passion just a few days before. His tone, his expression, even the arm she clutched, were iron-hard, and brought back such vivid reminders of the weeks following their marriage that the old Gabriella would have crumbled in the face of it. But that pale, intimidated creature had had so little left to lose that fighting to hold on to it had been a lost cause from the start.

Today's woman, though, had seen a glimpse of paradise and wasn't about to forfeit it willingly. ''You did!'' she said heatedly. ''You told me the apron I found in the kitchen had been left behind by a housekeeper when you knew it really belonged to Willow.''

''If that's the case, this is the first I knew of it and I made an honest *mistake,* which is a whole hell of a lot different from telling an outright lie. But the fact that you'd allow so insignificant an item to be instrumental in eroding what little trust you have in me merely proves my point.''

''It need never have been an issue, if you'd been up front with me in the first place and told me Willow lived here for a month. But you couldn't bring yourself to do that, could you?'' She let go of his sleeve with fastidious distaste. ''And you want to know why? Because you do such a good job of deceiving *yourself,* and I am disappointed beyond words to discover you could be such a coward.''

His face flushed dull red, his eyes sparked blue fury.

"Don't push your luck, Gabriella. I'd flatten any man who dared call me that."

"Sorry if the truth hurts, but that hardly changes it. If you'd dared to face up to what Willow has really been after for months now, things would never have come to such a pitiful pass tonight."

He shrugged. "Pitiful's the word, all right, if a pair of earrings or an apron can bring about this much damage!"

"I'm not talking about material things like jewelry, or having some other woman make herself at home here. For heaven's sake, you're not a stupid man, even if you sometimes act that way. At some level, you must have known that her feelings for you crossed the line from professional to personal a long time ago."

"Not necessarily. I don't go around assuming every woman I clap eyes on has the hots for me."

"Oh, spare me, Max! You kissed her and from all accounts, she kissed you back. Are you trying to tell me you thought she was being *motherly?*"

Even before he replied, she knew she'd scored a point from the way his lips thinned into a severe line. "At the time, she agreed with me that it was a mistake best forgotten."

Gabriella shook her head despairingly. "How is it that you are so ready to believe what another woman tells you despite evidence that's she either lying or deluding herself, yet you refuse to accept that I mean it from the bottom of my heart and soul when I say I love you, and everything I've ever done, ill-conceived or otherwise, proves it?"

"You call walking out on me after only six months of marriage proof that you...care about me?"

"It's because I cared that I left. I couldn't stand watching us destroy each other. And how come a man who claims he isn't a coward can't bring himself to say the word 'love'?''

"Because I don't believe in tossing it around as a Band-Aid solution every time something goes wrong in a relationship. It takes more than that to hold a couple together.''

"Yes, it does," she said. "But love also goes a long way toward keeping a marriage intact when the going gets rough.''

"Then I guess that explains why ours is such a mess.''

He tossed the words at her almost glibly, but she wasn't about to let him get away with that. "It might not be in such bad shape if you were as quick to recognize your own weaknesses as you are mine.''

"And how do you figure that?''

"You make much of my not being able to trust you, but the fact is, you're afraid to trust yourself.''

"I am not!''

"Yes, you are," she said defiantly. "You're afraid to look into your own heart.''

"Bull!''

"Really? Then answer me this." She cupped his jaw and forced him to meet her gaze. "Have you ever, for a single moment, loved me?''

His glance veered away, past her and out to the dark waters of the strait. And she knew, if he could, he'd have disappeared into them and never surfaced again. Anything to avoid having to deal with a subject she'd never laid bare to him before because she hadn't wanted to put him on the spot, and she supposed, if she were honest, because she'd been afraid to hear how he might respond.

But the way she saw it, they were at such a low point

that she might as well face all her demons and have done with.

"Well?" she said. "I've put my pride on the line and asked the question, Max. Do you have the guts to answer it honestly?"

# CHAPTER NINE

THE strain of maintaining appearances for those last hours of her parents' visit was worse than all that in the days which had gone before. Not that anyone made specific reference to the previous night's closing act at the hotel; in fact, the morning routine they'd established began as usual. After Max left for the office, Gabriella served oven-warm brioches with fruit preserves, then her father took a swim in the pool while she and her mother lingered over coffee.

They were barely settled under the terrace umbrella, though, when Maria observed, ''You have dark circles under your eyes, darling. Did you not sleep well?''

''Not particularly.'' Gabriella pushed her fingers through her hair dispiritedly. ''I miss you already, Mama. The time's gone by so quickly and we haven't taken you to half the places we'd planned to show you. You've spent most of your time here in the penthouse.''

''But we've seen how you live. When I'm home again, I'll be able to picture you here with your husband, and I'll remember the happy times we've shared with you.''

''Happy? Oh, Mama!'' She'd promised herself she wouldn't cry, but trying to hold back the tears was as impossible as trying to get Max to say he loved her. ''You could hardly have helped hearing us after you'd gone to bed last night. The French doors were wide open, and I think half the people in this city probably must have heard.''

''So?''

"So you know that Max and I are anything but happy!"

"I know that two people can fight as fiercely as they love. I know, too, that sometimes the love can become poisoned and seem more like hate."

"And this doesn't upset you?"

Her mother took a sip of coffee before replying, "It would upset me more if I saw only apathy between you and your husband. Passion doesn't kill a marriage, my daughter. Only indifference can do that."

How true! Max's dismissal of her question, his bruising detachment when at last he'd joined her in bed, had spelled out quite clearly that, as far as he was concerned, their marriage was dead. The poison, as her mother put it, had been left too long to do its treacherous work.

Her mother stroked her hand lovingly. "You'll make up, as soon as we're gone, Gabriella. It puts a strain on any marriage always to have to be on one's best behavior in front of guests."

"It's more than that, Mama. I'm afraid the truth is that Max and I are too used to living apart. We don't know how to be a real couple anymore."

"Then stay at home. Remind him all over again how it is to come home at night to find his wife waiting."

But sound though the advice was, and much though Gabriella would have loved to follow it, it came too late.

"I suppose you'll be leaving right after your parents are gone?" Max had said to her, just that morning.

She'd been in bed still when he'd come out of the bathroom wearing only a pair of white briefs. His hair, still damp from the shower, lay flatter than usual against his well-shaped head. His jaw was smooth as silk, his eyes a stunning blue against his sun-dark skin.

He strode past the foot of the bed to fling open the long windows and as he passed, she picked up on a faint trace of his aftershave: Davidoff's Cool Water—a fitting choice for a man who was, above all, coolly contained on the outside regardless of whatever demons haunted him within.

"I might as well," she'd replied, covertly watching as he crossed the room again to the tray on his valet where he kept his wallet and other small personal items. He looked utterly beautiful, utterly masculine. And utterly remote. "I've got a ten week overseas assignment coming up, starting in Tokyo next Wednesday, and I like to leave myself a couple of days to catch up with the time change."

"Sounds like a brutal schedule."

"I'll be at my usual hotel in Paris by the end of September, but if you need to get in touch with me before then, my agent—"

"I know how to reach you, should something come up. What I was going to say is, if you want to hang out here an extra day to catch your breath, you're welcome to do so."

"Thank you, but there's nothing to be gained in my staying. I'll put everything back the way I found it and be out of your hair by Monday at the latest."

He picked up his watch, the same stainless-steel Rolex he'd worn since before he met her. For all his millions, he was not an ostentatious man and though he was often generous to a fault with others, his personal tastes ran along rather austere lines.

His next words illustrated the point with chilling accuracy. "I was going to talk to you about that," he'd said, snapping the bracelet closed around his wrist. "You ought to arrange to have all that stuff you left behind the first time you took off shipped to your place in Rome. It's yours anyway, and you probably have more use for it than

I ever will. In fact, I don't know why you haven't claimed it before now.''

She could have told him the reason, if she'd thought he was the least bit interested in hearing her say, *Because I secretly hoped we'd find our way back to each other, and enjoy it together.*

But he'd laid to rest any chance of that happening when he'd turned away from her question the night before. *I fail to see where love comes into the picture,* he'd replied, and the emotional distance he'd put between them since bore out the sincerity of his belief.

''I'll arrange to have it removed as soon as possible,'' she said, and turned her face away before he saw the misery she knew must be obvious even to the most casual observer.

*I will remember this moment for the rest of my life,* she'd thought, closing her eyes but unable to shut out the picture emblazoned in her mind of the sun spearing the room to burnish his shoulders, and highlight his profile in such a way that his lashes formed dusky shadows on his cheeks.

Sublimely indifferent to her misery, he'd strolled into his dressing room—a respite she gravely needed—and returned a couple of minutes later wearing dark gray trousers and a white dress shirt. ''Would you like to take your folks out for their last night here?'' he asked, sliding a burgundy-and-blue silk tie under the shirt collar. ''I'll be happy to reserve a table somewhere.''

''No,'' she said hurriedly. She'd had enough of being in the public eye for one week, on top of which she'd seen how her parents' energy, particularly her father's, faded by the end of the day. ''I'm sure they'd prefer to spend a quiet evening here with just us before they undertake the long journey home tomorrow, but I'll understand if you'd find that too difficult and prefer to stay away.''

He'd fixed her in a somber gaze. ''I have no quarrel with your parents, Gabriella. I like and respect them both, and I'm no more interested in upsetting them than you are. If a quiet evening with just the four of us is what you think they'd like, that's what they'll get.''

''Thank you.''

Her mouth had been trembling so hard, she'd barely been able to articulate the words. Noticing, he'd given the Windsor knot in his tie a final inspection, then hooked his hands on his hips and blown out a breath. ''I like you, too, you know, and for what it's worth, I'm disappointed we weren't able to work things out.''

''Gabriella?'' With a start, she realized her mother was observing her with all the wisdom that came of having weathered seventy-odd years of more turmoil and heart-ache than any one person should be asked to bear.

''How do you do it, Mama?'' she asked, struggling to keep her emotions under control. ''How is it that you've never lost faith in yourself? How have you managed to get up and face another day, when so often you must have thought you had nothing left worth living for?''

''Never lost faith?'' Her mother smiled. ''Oh, my dar-ling, if you only knew how many times I was ready to give up! When your brother was killed, I wished I had died with him. I blamed your father for not having taken us to a safer place until the troubles were over. But he wouldn't desert his country and when it came right down to it, I couldn't desert him. I loved him too much, just as you love your Max. And in the end, I was rewarded. I was blessed with you—a beautiful daughter when I thought my child-bearing years were behind me. It's true that good things come to those who wait, Gabriella. The secret lies in not giving up the fight, and trusting in the healing power of love."

She spoke with such calm assurance that Gabriella was almost persuaded to believe her. A whole weekend alone with Max stretched ahead: two full days and two long nights. Only a week or so ago, when they'd finally dared let down their defenses, they'd found their way back to each other in less than an hour. Surely, if she put her whole heart and soul into it, she could pull off another such miracle?

But not without Max's cooperation and that, she discovered, was not forthcoming.

"I hoped I'd be able to take the morning off and drive you to the airport tomorrow," he told her parents, that night at dinner, "but I just got word that clients I've been expecting are flying in from Geneva tonight and it looks as if I'm going to be completely tied up with them for the next couple of days."

"We can order a taxi," Gabriella said, doing her best to swallow this latest blow to her hopes.

"No need. You can take my car instead. It'll be more convenient, especially with all the errands you have to run between now and Monday."

Good grief, he could hardly wait to be rid of her! "But if you're entertaining clients," she said, "surely you'll need it yourself?"

"No." Impervious to the pain his words inflicted, he calmly helped himself to more salad. "I've chartered a helicopter to fly us to Whistler for a few days of golf."

"When do you plan to leave?" she asked him, after they were in bed.

He yawned and stretched, then clasped his hands behind his head and closed his eyes. "Tomorrow, as soon as the morning meetings are over."

So much for a weekend of miracles! "Does that mean I won't see you again after tonight?"

"Not if you take off on Monday as planned."

"And if I don't?"

His eyes opened a crack. "I thought you had to be in Tokyo by Wednesday?"

"There's a lot to do here, between now and then. I could always wait an extra day."

"Why, Gabriella?" he said, slewing a weary glance her way. "What would be the point?"

Stung, she said tartly, "I know you're glad this entire charade is into its final act, but you might at least try to pretend a little regret that it's not ending as well as we'd hoped!"

"Regret, like guilt, is a waste of energy."

She wanted to shake him! "How can you lie there so passively with our marriage in its final death throes, and not feel *something?*"

His chest rose in a massive sigh. "What do you want me to say? We gave it our best shot and still managed to screw up big-time, and I refuse to keep on doing it—to me or to you. I feel like a big enough fool, as it is."

"No more than I do!" she retorted, deeply angered by his attitude. "I must have been crazy to believe you ever intended to make a serious effort to reconcile. Why would you, when you have Willow waiting to fill my shoes? She's obviously so much better suited to the job of catering to your needs than I ever was."

"*Crazy?*" he echoed mockingly. "Add *jealous* and *suspicious* to the list, and you're finally coming close to discovering what I've suspected all along—you're the over-the-top star in your own tragic soap opera!"

"Am I, Max? Or is it more that I'm coming too close to the truth for your comfort? Because the fact remains that you shut me out when I tried to be a wife to you, but you let her in.''

''You didn't stick around long enough to learn the first thing about being a wife! We never took the time to get to know each other at the start, to find out what, if anything, we shared in common—besides good sex, that is— and we're still making the same mistake now. And whether you believe it or not, at least I know Willow well enough to recognize she's not what I want. Whereas with you—!''

Frustrated, he jerked half upright, yanked his pillow from behind his head and dealt it a savage punch, then stuffed it under his shoulder and angled himself away from her.

''What about me?'' Furious herself, she glared at his back. ''Come on, Max, you're so fixated on spitting out the truth at all costs, so speak your piece. After all, it might be your last chance ever to tell me exactly what you think of me!''

''Never mind,'' he said, gazing stubbornly at the window. ''I won't be part of this anymore. I'm tired of trying to separate fact from fiction, truth from fantasy. And I'm tired of rehashing history. This isn't yesterday, or two years ago. This is now—and it's about us. About how we haven't learned a damned thing from past mistakes, and just keep repeating them. And I take full responsibility for it. If I'd followed my instincts and turfed you out of my room that first night, we wouldn't be in this mess now.''

''How noble of you—and how hypocritical!''

She sensed rather than saw the indignation sweep over him. ''What the devil's *that* supposed to mean?''

''Your instinct was to take what I was so willing to give, and no questions asked! You welcomed me with open arms.''

He bolted up from the bed. "You took me by surprise!"

"And you simply *took* me! Very willingly, I might add."

"You're a lovely, passionate woman, Gabriella, and hard to resist when you put your mind to it," he said, slumping back against the pillows. "I've never denied that, anymore than I have that, physically at least, we're ideally suited. Too bad that's *all* we have going for us, because by itself it's not enough to float a successful marriage, and any doubts we might have entertained on that score have been laid to rest with a vengeance in the last twenty-four hours."

"Really?" she taunted him. "I think it has more to do with the fact that there might be a great deal more to our relationship than you're willing to admit, because that would involve your looking honestly into your heart, and you're afraid of what you might find. And you know what? That sets me free to go forward without you."

"I see." He half turned and regarded her coldly. "And the point of your little homily is?"

She swallowed the tears that suddenly threatened because he was right: regret was useless, and guilt a burden she didn't deserve. She'd done penance enough for past sins. "That I'm accepting failure—mine *and* yours!— and I'm ready to close the book on us. I'll begin divorce proceedings as soon as possible. You'll never have to see me again after tomorrow morning."

If she'd hoped that might shock him into realizing he was throwing away something precious, he quickly disabused her of the idea. "At least you have the decency to be up front about leaving this time, instead of leaving a note."

"Yes," she said. "I'm no longer that insecure, homesick little bride trying to adjust to a new life in a new country and desperate to win her husband's approval at any cost. I've grown up, Max, and I think it's time you did the same.''

*''Huh?''*

If she hadn't been too emotionally battered to feel anything but a blessed numbness, she'd have found his thunderstruck expression comical. "You heard," she said. "Instead of lecturing me about letting go of the past, try practicing what you preach. Stop hanging on to old resentments and using them to justify your present choices. Maybe if you can learn to do that, you'll find sharing your life with someone isn't such a burdensome undertaking, after all.'' She pulled the sheet up to her chin and edged closer to her side of the bed to give him as wide a berth as possible. "Who knows? You might even learn to be truly happy one day.''

"You speak from personal experience, no doubt!''

She flinched at the biting sarcasm. "Not yet, but I'm not giving up. I'm willing to try again, and the next time, I'll choose more wisely and get it right.''

"I wish you luck.''

"Luck doesn't enter into it. I've done my best to right all the wrongs that caused so much trouble and damage to our marriage, and whether or not you believe it, I've learned from the experience.''

"Have you really, Gabriella?'' he sneered. "And what is it, exactly, that you've learned?''

She gazed at the reflection of the pool shimmering on the ceiling and thought a moment before saying calmly, "Mostly that it takes two to make a couple. One person can't do it on her own, no matter how hard she tries. In our case, I want to be happily married, but you don't. So, I'm cutting my losses and moving on in the hope that, someday, I'll find a man willing to share more than just his bed with me.''

Brave words spoken with commendable assurance, but *so* difficult to abide by the next morning as she stood in the penthouse foyer, watching as Max made his farewells to her parents and knowing that, when he finally turned to her, it would be for another last goodbye.

He took her hands and for a long aching moment, looked into her eyes. ''Well,'' he said, his voice a little rough, perhaps even a little uncertain, as though the words were hard come by, ''don't let them work you too hard and stay safe, okay?''

''Okay.'' She must have seemed composed enough on the outside, because neither her mother nor her father appeared to notice anything amiss, but inside she was dying—*dying!*—an inch at a time, in slow and torturous agony.

''And start taking better care of yourself.'' His thumbs traced warm little circles over the backs of her hands. He bent his head, pressed a kiss to her forehead, smudged another to the corner of her mouth. ''Make sure you eat properly. I hate to see you looking so thin.''

For him to be killing her with kindness now was insupportable and she knew a swift and fervent urge to punish him. Before she lost courage, she threaded her fingers through his thick, black hair and kissed him back, a deliberately slow, intimate kiss full on the lips. One which dared him to rebuff her.

She angled her face so that her lashes fluttered against his cheek, and let her eyes drift closed. She drank in the scent of him; the taste and texture of his beautiful, sexy mouth. She imprinted her body against his one last time, and had the small satisfaction of hearing the sharply indrawn breath he wasn't able to suppress.

"Be good to yourself," she whispered when at last she pulled away. Then, unable to bear seeing him leave, she turned and ran up the stairs. Once inside their bedroom, she leaned against the closed door and let the tears run free in silent, shuddering sobs.

Four hours later, she was weeping again, this time as she watched her parents pass through the security gates at the airport. As she had several times in the previous two years, she would visit them whenever her work took her close to her native home, but right at that moment, she felt as if she was being abandoned by the only people left in the world who cared whether she lived or died.

As if he knew it, too, her father had almost broken down when it came to their parting. "Remember we love you and that, however much other circumstances might change, you will always be our daughter," he'd muttered, enveloping her in a bone-crushing hug. "Remember, too, that we are only a phone call away any time that you need us."

Reliving the words in her mind as she drove out of the airport and merged with the heavy traffic heading toward downtown Vancouver, she thought it unlikely that he'd been taken in for a moment by the lengths to which she'd gone to portray a happily married woman. Instead, he'd simply played the game, along with everyone else.

Would he accept news of her divorce with equal forbearance? she wondered. Would her mother? Or would they be disappointed to learn she lacked the tenacity with which they'd clung to their ideals and dreams?

Perhaps if she'd been less involved in her thoughts and more tuned in to her surroundings, she'd have seen the commotion taking place outside the convenience store a few yards away from where she'd stopped for a red light. She'd have realized the danger before it was too late, and taken the simple precaution of hitting the automatic door and window lock buttons on the console.

But by the time the car's front passenger door was suddenly wrenched open and a body hurled itself inside, it was too late to do anything but stare in horrified fascination, first at the long, vicious blade of the knife resting in uncomfortable proximity to her neck, then at the sullen face of the young thug huddled next to her.

"Out!" he snarled, both his tone and the gesture which went with it indicating she was expected to vacate Max's sleek, expensive imported sedan and leave it to tender mercies of her uninvited passenger.

A distant part of her mind told her she would be wise to obey; that even a life as miserable as hers was more valuable than a mere car. But the emotional paralysis which had gripped her ever since she'd realized her marriage was over left her curiously indifferent to anything but the fact that, even though he didn't love her, his car was one thing Max did prize highly.

So, "I'm afraid I can't possibly do that," she said. "It isn't my car and my husband is already annoyed enough with me that I shudder to think how he'd react if I simply turned it over to the first person who asked."

The youth—for certainly he couldn't have been more than fifteen or sixteen—cast a hunted look over his shoulder. Following his glance, Gabriella saw a small crowd converging on the car. She heard the distant wail of sirens coming closer.

So did the boy. "Start burning rubber, lady!" he snarled. "I'm in one hell of a hurry."

"Certainly. Where would you like me to take you?"

Amazed, she realized that although her hands were shaking, she'd voiced the question with all the aplomb of a duchess offering afternoon tea to a titled guest.

Her uncouth passenger seemed equally taken aback, though only briefly. Mouthing an obscenity, he brought the cold steel terrifyingly close to her throat and grasped a rough fistful of her hair. "You want to see your old man again, hang a right at the intersection and head for the freeway. And save trying to be funny. In case you haven't noticed, I'm not laughing."

Still in a trance, she shifted gear and followed his instructions to the letter. Tires squealing, the big car surged forward just as flashing lights appeared in the distance.

# CHAPTER TEN

KEEPING his attention where it belonged—namely on the three overseas clients currently poring over spreadsheets and tossing around figures which ran into millions—was difficult when the only movie playing in Max's head was Gabriella.

Saying goodbye had been a lot tougher than he'd anticipated. At the last, he'd been swamped with doubts. The uncomplicated future he'd thought he wanted shone less brightly. No matter how he added them up, those things he'd always considered important suddenly weren't enough to hold the fabric of his life together.

The idea that he might be losing his taste for business was shocking enough, but the real eye-opener was, he didn't much care. For years, he'd been driven by ambition, thrived on success, treasured the freedom which allowed him to go wherever and whenever the greatest challenge presented itself.

But how many awards did a man need before he knew he'd climbed to the top? How many rivals did he outbid before his competitive spirit lost its edge?

As for the highly touted freedom—what the hell did *that* amount to if, at the end of it all, the only thing he had to come home to was a penthouse so devoid of life that it too often felt more like a tomb than a home, and the only person who even cared whether he lived or died was the assistant who planned his itineraries and penciled in his appointments?

Which brought him to his other big problem. Willow.

Distracted, he rolled back his chair and went to the cloth-draped table at the far end of the boardroom where coffee and pastries were laid out.

*I should have insisted she pack up and have done with, instead of agreeing to let her work out her month's notice,* he thought irritably, pausing before a highly polished coffee urn—silver, probably, but it didn't make the stuff inside taste any better, so who the devil cared! *She'll be underfoot every time I turn around, trying to make herself indispensable and prove I can't do without her.*

As though on cue, she appeared at the door and with ostentatious stealth made her way to where he stooped over the table, stirring cream into his coffee.

"Sorry to intrude," she whispered, her breath leaving an unpleasantly damp cloud over his ear, "but you have a visitor."

"Not now," he snapped in a low voice. Cripes, had she lost her mind, interrupting negotiations at such a critical stage? Just because he was somewhat disenchanted with business at the moment didn't mean he was ready to watch the last six months' work get flushed down the drain!

"This can't wait, Max. There's a police officer outside, a Detective Janssen, and he's very insistent on speaking to you in person."

*"Police?"* He snapped his mouth closed on the word and cast a furtive glance around, glad to see he hadn't been overheard and that the clients were still engrossed in the graphs and blueprints spread out in front of them.

Sensing something untoward must be afoot though, his vice president joined him at the coffee table. "What's up?"

"Seems I've got the police breathing down my neck on some matter." Max shrugged, more annoyed than disturbed. "Hold down the fort while I check it out, okay? We've pretty much covered the main points here anyway, so run the video on the Indonesian project if I'm not back before you wrap up, and I'll join you for lunch in the executive dining room."

Making his excuses to the clients, he then followed Willow out of the room. "If this is about an overdue parking ticket, someone's head's going to roll!" he warned her, striding down the hall to his office.

"If it were that minor, I wouldn't have interrupted the meeting," she said reproachfully. "But I got the impression it was something rather more serious than a traffic infraction."

Eyeing the plainclothes officer waiting by his desk, Max decided she was probably right. "Sorry to be the bearer of bad news," Detective Janssen began, once the introductions were out of the way, "but there's been an incident involving an automobile registered in your name."

*Gabriella had taken his car to the airport!* The first tendrils of fear spiraled through Max's bloodstream. "Incident?" he repeated hollowly. "Or accident?"

"Your car was stolen, Mr. Logan, and used as the getaway vehicle in a botched attempt at armed robbery."

Reaction set in, leaving him light-headed with relief. Gabriella was famously careless about locking up when she parked the car. Couldn't even recall where she'd left it, half the time. Once, she'd come out of a shop on south Granville and spent an hour looking for it before discovering it had been towed away because she'd left it in a restricted zone. Remembering, Max almost smiled. "Is that all?"

Janssen regarded him gravely. "Not quite, I'm afraid. Did you loan your car to anyone this morning?"

"Yes. My wife used it to take her parents to the airport." He did laugh then. "I hope you're not implying she tried to stick up a bank!"

"On the contrary. Whoever was driving your car this morning was taken hostage in the incident."

The blood roared in Max's ears. Unthinkingly, he grabbed a fistful of the man's shirtfront and shook him like a dog with a rabbit in its jaws. "What do you mean, she was taken hostage? What the devil are you trying to tell me?"

The detective calmly pried himself loose and straightened his tie. "According to witnesses, she appeared to argue with the suspect, even though he threatened her with a knife. It's likely he wanted the car and she refused to give it up."

*"She did what?"* Max dropped into his chair, his heart free-falling in horrific slow motion.

"She refused to turn over the keys. So he took her with him. She was last seen driving south over the Oak Street Bridge, with him holding the knife to her throat."

All at once, Max felt as if he were swimming in thick, gluey oil; as if the whole, ugly world were closing in and squeezing the life out of him.

Just that morning, she'd kissed him. He'd tasted her incredible mouth, felt her long, lithe body pressed up against his, looked into her shimmering green eyes. And told himself he was well rid of her, when what he should have done was tell her that she was right. He *was* a coward! He didn't have the guts to face up to his feelings for her.

And now some half-crazed thug on the run had her—and just what he planned to do with her when she'd outlived her usefulness made Max's blood run cold.

"I realize this is shocking news, Mr. Logan," Janssen

said sympathetically, "but if it's any comfort, we have roadblocks set up. They won't get far. And with her behind the wheel instead of him, the odds are that excessive speed won't be a factor."

*That was supposed to comfort him, when a maniac was holding a knife to her lovely throat?* "I'm hardly concerned about a speeding ticket right now," he ground out hoarsely.

"Naturally not. What I meant to say is that safety—"

But whatever slim comfort the detective had been about to dish up next was interrupted by the chirping of his cell phone. Pacing to the window, he unclipped the instrument from his belt and answered.

The few words he spoke were too low to be overheard but the conversation was mercifully brief and when he turned again to Max, his face looked a little less somber. "Good news. The car's been found and the suspect apprehended."

Max could barely bring himself to ask, "And my wife?"

"She's being brought in also."

*"In?"* he barked. "In *where?* To a hospital? A morgue?"

"To police headquarters, Mr. Logan. She appears not to have been harmed. If you like, I can take you down there to be with her while she's questioned."

"Oh, I'd like," he said grimly. In fact, there were a number of things he'd like, and right at the top of his list was a raging need to see for himself that she hadn't been hurt. Then he'd like to spank her delectable backside for being such an idiot!

Yet when he was led into the room where she waited, he sagged in the doorway and simply feasted his eyes on the sight of her perched on a bench next to a police-woman, and sipping tea out of a paper cup.

When she saw him, she put the tea aside and slowly stood up, looking for all the world like a kid about to be punished for stealing from the cookie jar. "I'm very sorry, Max," she said, all big stricken eyes and quivering mouth. "I'm afraid your car's a bit the worse for wear but I'll pay for the repairs."

"You'd better believe it," he said thickly, covering the distance between them and sweeping her into his arms. "I'm going to take every last cent out of your beautiful hide!"

Then, to his eternal shame and embarrassment, he started bawling like a kid. Fat, sloppy tears dripped into her hair. And as if that wasn't humiliation enough, great jarring sobs took him by surprise and tore through him.

He wished he could fall between the cracks in the floor! He couldn't remember the last time he'd cried, but he thought it was when he was about four and found a dead squirrel in the driveway of his parents' house.

He hadn't cried at his mother's funeral fifteen years later, or when his father drank himself to death within six months of her passing, because grown men didn't cry. They coped at all costs. They kept their feelings bottled up inside and went toe-to-toe with the whole world before they'd allow anything to break them.

"Jeez, Gabriella, the things you do to me," he muttered, struggling to get a grip on his emotions.

"I'm sorry," she said again, and he realized she was sobbing into his shirtfront. And shaking like a leaf.

Blinking furiously, he fished a handkerchief out of his breast pocket, blew his nose, and wrapped his arms more firmly around her. Seeming to decide she was superfluous to the reunion, the policewoman let the door click shut behind her as she left the room.

Grateful for the privacy, Max led Gabriella to the bench and pulled her down on his lap. "It's over, sweetheart," he murmured unsteadily. "I'm here, and you're safe."

She hiccuped softly and buried her face against his chest, and for a while there was no need for words. It was enough that they were together. Enough that he could run his hand up and down her spine and know she was in one piece. Enough that he could feel the pulse beating beneath her jaw, and feel her rib cage expand with every breath.

Eventually she grew calmer and lifted her head to shoot an embarrassed glance his way. "I must look a mess!"

"You look like something the cat dragged in, and you're the most beautiful sight in the world," he murmured, his gaze scouring her face. Then he saw the angry red welt on the side of her neck; touched it with the tip of his finger and saw her wince. "And I'm going to kill the bastard who did this to you."

"Oh, Max, he's just a boy and he was so frightened."

"Was he really! Well, I was bloody terrified!"

"He made a mistake, and I know what that's like. You start out with something small and before you know it, things have snowballed out of control, and it's too late to put a stop to them."

He rolled his eyes in disbelief. "You'll be telling me next you feel sorry for the little creep."

"I do." She touched her forehead to his. "When I first met you, all I wanted was to kiss you. But the better I got to know you, the less I was satisfied with just that, so I tried to seduce you, and we both know where that led."

"The two situations hardly compare."

"Don't they?" She reared back a little and inspected

him soberly. "Didn't you feel you'd been taken hostage by me and coerced into a situation you didn't want?"

"For crying out loud, Gabriella…!" He leaned his head against the wall and clapped a hand to his brow. "Listen to me. This kid is ruthless enough to wield a knife, rob a store, and take a helpless woman prisoner. In my book, that makes him a criminal. A menace to decent society. And I'm going to have them throw the book at him for what he's put you through this morning!"

She drew her thumb over his mouth. "The way you're carrying on, anyone would think you cared about me."

"Jeez, woman, I *love* you!"

She stared at him, her eyes wide green pools of shock, while the words bounced off the stark walls of the room and ricocheted back to haunt him. "What did you say?"

Pretty shaken up himself, he stared right back. Having this conversation take place in an interrogation room at the local cop shop hardly fit his idea of romantic ambience, but the moment was right, and he'd put off baring his soul long enough. "I love you," he repeated sheepishly.

He kind of thought she'd tell him she loved him, too. After all, she'd been implying it long enough! Instead, she slid off his lap and put a safe six feet of space between them. "No, you don't. Not really. You're just grateful and relieved that I'm not hurt."

"Oh, I'm a lot more than just that!" He shoved himself off the bench and stalked her across the room. "I came close to losing you this morning, and I'm not talking about us going our separate ways or leading separate lives. Out of the blue, I was confronted by the very real possibility that you could have been killed—that there'd be no going back to try again, no making up and starting over.

No occasional long-distance phone calls just to touch base. No more you.''

He swallowed, afraid his emotions were going to seize up and make an ass of him again. ''I couldn't handle it, Gabriella. It's as simple as that. So maybe you're right, and I don't love you. But if that's the case, then please explain to me why I didn't want to wake up tomorrow knowing you might not be part of my world anymore. Tell me why I felt as if someone had blown a hole clean through my heart.''

Detective Janssen poked his head around the door and spared her having to answer. ''If you feel up to it, Mrs. Logan, we'd like to get a statement from you.''

''Of course.'' She swayed across the room with that inbred elegance that had captivated Max from the first. ''Go back to work, Max,'' she said, over her shoulder. ''I'll be fine by myself.''

''Like hell, you will!'' He caught up with her in three strides flat. ''I'm staying here to take you home when you're done, and that is *not* something that's up for discussion.''

Max had closed the wooden shutters over the windows, leaving the bedroom full of pale, filtered light. The pillow beneath her head was cool and smooth, the light quilt covering her, soft and clean.

*The boy's hand had been filthy, his nails bitten down to the quicks.*

''Try to sleep,'' Max had said, stroking the hair off her face and dropping a kiss on her forehead. ''We'll talk later, have a quiet dinner together. I'll order something in, open a bottle of wine. But right now, you need to get some rest.''

*''Stupid, rich cow,''* the boy had spat, when she'd tried

*to persuade him to give himself up. "What do you know about living on the street? When was the last time you picked through a back alley Dumpster to find something to fill your belly?"*

"Take her home," the kind detective had said, after she'd given her statement. "She's in shock, but otherwise okay. We don't need to keep her here."

Max had led her out into the warm blue afternoon, one arm firmly around her waist. A shiny new Lincoln Continental stood in the parking lot. Opening the door, he poured her into the front seat. Even went so far as to buckle her into her belt, as if he really did care about keeping her safe.

"Where did you get the car?" she'd asked listlessly.

"I leased it. Made a call while you were busy with Janssen and arranged to have it waiting for us after you'd given your statement."

*"Some ride you got here," the boy had said enviously, running his hand over the car's rich leather upholstery. "Bet you just take it all for granted, though. Anything you want, your old man goes out and slaps down the money, and it's yours. Easy come, easy go, right down the line."*

"You don't have to take me to the penthouse," she'd told Max, knowing how he probably hated the idea now that the whole horrible business with the police was over, and he'd seen for himself that she was okay. "I can stay in a hotel."

He'd stopped with his hand on the ignition key and stared at her. "If that's meant to be funny, sweetheart, you should know I'm in no mood to be entertained."

"Oh, what a coincidence!" she'd gasped, involuntary peals of laughter streaming from her mouth and filling the plush interior of the car with ripple after ripple of merriment. "That's more or less what that poor young boy said when I asked him where he wanted me to take him."

*"As far away as I can get from this lousy place."*

*"But what about your mother? Won't she be worried? Won't she wonder where you are?"*

*He'd let out an embittered croak of amusement and wiped the back of his hand across his mouth. His wrist was as slender as a girl's. "As long as she gets her daily fix, my old lady don't give a rat's ass about me or anyone else."*

"What were you thinking of, all the time he held you at knifepoint?" Max had asked, during the drive back to the penthouse.

"That I was going to die and wouldn't have to divorce you, after all. I'd be your late wife, instead of your ex— a much more respectable way to end things."

She'd meant to sound carelessly sophisticated, to be the woman she so often portrayed in her work—untouched, remote, in control—but try though she might to keep her cool exterior firmly in place, inside she'd come unspooled. Tears had plopped off the end of her nose; her voice had quavered like a child's. A deep, aching pit had opened up where her stomach used to be.

"It's going to be all right, sweetheart," Max had consoled her, folding her hand in his. "I'll look after you. No one's ever again going to hurt you or frighten you like that."

*"Put away the knife," she'd urged the boy, when the roadblock had loomed up ahead and flashing lights from a trio of police cars had closed in behind. "Explain you haven't eaten in days, that you have no place to live, that you were desperate. Maybe they'll understand and get you the help you need."*

*"You're a freakin' fool, you know that?" the boy had*

*jeered, but his eyes had been wide with fear. "Cops don't understand, and the only one who's going to help me is me. Hit the brakes. I'm bailing out."*

*When she hadn't immediately responded, his voice had risen to a scream. "Stop the freakin' car, I said!"*

*She'd slammed both feet on the brake pedal. Felt the heavy car fishtail perilously out of control, then rock terrifyingly from side to side before spinning like a donut across two lanes toward a two-foot-high cement divider separating her from oncoming traffic.*

*She'd wrestled with the steering wheel, heard the endless squeal of tires, smelled the trail of smoking rubber on the pavement, seen the roadblock rearing up, huge and deadly and then, at the last moment before impact, the passenger door flying open and the boy's fragile body, curled up and catapulting into space, then rolling like a ball into the deep ditch.*

*And she'd screamed until her throat stung. In terror for his life, and for her own…!*

"Gabriella, wake up!" Max's urgent voice penetrated the horror. His strong arms lifted the tangle of quilt from around her legs. His hands—those magical, wonderful hands which knew so well how to thrill her with pleasure—wiped away the sweat pouring down her face. "You were dreaming, honey."

"The boy!" she whimpered, that final scene still vivid in her mind. "They took him away in an ambulance!"

"Janssen phoned while you were sleeping. Apart from a few cuts and bruises, none of them serious, the kid's going to be fine. Well enough to be arraigned first thing Monday morning." He plumped up the pillows and helped her to sit up, "Sweetheart, forget about him and start worrying about yourself. From what I've heard, you're going to be pretty sore tomorrow. If you'd rammed head-on into that roadblock, you'd be lying in a hospital bed now. Luckily, the car scraped by with only a glancing blow on the passenger side.''

''Can it be fixed—the car, I mean?''

''Who gives a rip, one way or the other? It's replaceable. You're not.'' He pinched the bridge of his nose and briefly closed his eyes as if a thousand tiny hammers were pounding in his skull. ''How are *you* feeling?''

She rotated her shoulders cautiously. ''I have to admit, I'm feeling a bit stiff.''

''Hardly surprising, but I happen to have the perfect remedy.'' He glanced at the bedside clock Willow had made such a point of mentioning she'd bought for him. Funny how, in light of the morning's events, everything *she*'d said and done seemed unimportant. ''I'll give you five minutes to get yourself into the hot tub.''

''I've already packed my swimsuit,'' Gabriella said.

''Then make do with your birthday suit. And don't look so fearful. I'm not such a lowlife that I'm going to ravish you in your weakened state.''

Well, of course he wouldn't! And she was ridiculous to be so bashful, when he already knew every inch of her body better than she did herself.

Still, she hesitated. The fact was, the balance of their relationship had shifted in the last few hours. Their roles weren't the same as they'd been that morning, or at any other time in their marriage. Real danger had entered the picture, acute enough that he'd told her, impulsively she was sure, that he loved her.

She'd always thought him too proud to succumb to anything as human as fear. That he wasn't didn't at all lessen him in her eyes; if anything it enhanced his appeal. But it also changed him. Suddenly, he was no longer the man she thought she knew.

Watching her and probably reading the doubts chasing through her mind, Max clicked his tongue impatiently and disappeared into the bathroom, returning a moment later with his thick terry-cloth robe slung over his arm. "Here. If modesty's an issue all of a sudden, wear this until you get down to the pool deck. I promise not to peek."

The prospect of having her aching body massaged by pulsing jets of hot water was tempting, no doubt about it. Certainly, she had no wish to remain in bed, prey to another nightmare rerun of the morning. "All right, you win."

He regarded her unsmilingly. "I usually do, sweetheart. Better learn to live with it!"

He'd ordered dinner—her favorite salad, and lobster in tarragon cream sauce with roasted endive, which she also loved—from a restaurant a couple of blocks away. It waited in the kitchen, packed in thermal containers to keep it at perfect serving temperature, along with a cheese board and a tray of petits fours.

Initially, he'd thought of doing the whole affair up in style in the formal dining room, but in the end had decided on something more intimate. He hadn't wanted her parked at one end of the long polished table, with him at the other. He wanted her close enough to touch. Wanted to be able to thread his fingers through her hair, and stroke his hand up her long, elegant leg. Wanted to hold her and kiss her, and tell her that when he'd said that morning that he loved her, he'd meant it.

So, while she showered and dressed, he started a fire in the living room to ward off the chill of the breeze floating in from the sea, and covered the coffee table with one of the antique hand-embroidered cloths she'd brought with her from Hungary. He hauled out the sterling-silver cutlery, and the Herend china so dear to her heart. Chilled a bottle of champagne and two wafer-thin flutes in a silver ice bucket. Slipped a couple of smoochy blues discs into the CD player and turned the volume low.

Then, as an afterthought, he cut a rose from the climber on the terrace and plunked it in a little crystal vase between the two candles burning on the table.

Still, she didn't appear.

What the devil could be keeping her?

Nervously, he paced the floor. Something about her had changed since the morning's incident, and he didn't just mean that she'd been shaken up. She'd withdrawn from everything around her, especially him.

If he didn't know better, he'd think she was afraid of him. And for the life of him he couldn't figure out why. What he *did* know was that he didn't like the way the foundation of their marriage seemed to be shifting under his feet yet again, just when he thought it had finally settled on solid ground.

Footsteps crossing from the stairs to the living room had him spinning around to find her standing haloed in the light from the foyer, and if he'd thought her beautiful before, he found her breathtaking now.

Her hair hung loose in a smooth pale curve that hid the ugly welt on her neck. Her skin glowed as if it were lit from inside with golden fire. The outfit she'd put on, a silky one-piece jumpsuit thing the color of a Rocky Mountain glacier, clung to her with enviable familiarity. She wore sandals webbed with leather straps so fine they resembled lace. Her jewelry consisted of little gold hoops at her ears and her wedding ring.

He hoped the latter boded well for the future.

"Have I kept you waiting?"

"If you have," he said, wondering why he had a lump

the size of a golf ball in his throat, and hoping like blazes he wasn't going to break down again, "it was worth every second."

She glided toward him, preceded by the merest hint of perfume, and allowed him to take her hands. He wanted to kiss her in the worst way, to crush her in his arms and never let her go.

But it as was if she'd surrounded herself with an invisible shield, one which dared him to try to get past, and he had to settle for giving her a peck on the cheek, then letting her go.

Stymied, he filled the champagne flutes. "Here's to us, Gabriella."

She inclined her head and touched the rim of her glass to his, but offered no answering toast, nor even a smile. Instead, she looked at his housekeeping efforts and said, "You've gone to a lot of trouble."

"You're worth it. I'm just sorry it took me this long to realize it."

Her gaze skittered away and settled on the fire.

Feeling slightly sick to his stomach, he said, "Honey, talk to me, please! Tell me what's put that introspective look in your eye."

Her shoulders tilted in a tiny shrug. "I'm wondering why you're here when I know you should be entertaining important clients."

"You're my wife, Gabriella. Where else would I be at a time like this?"

"I was your wife this morning, too, but that didn't stop you from planning to spend the weekend at Whistler."

He drew in a long breath and took a turn about the room before answering, "Maybe it's because I thought, given everything you've been through, that tonight you might need me more than my clients do. Or maybe it's that I've finally got my priorities in the proper order.''

''I don't believe priorities change that quickly. I think you're overreacting to an unfortunate incident and that you'll wake up tomorrow wishing you hadn't behaved quite so impulsively. I think,'' she finished carefully, ''that we might both live to regret your decision to abandon your overseas guests in my favor.''

''Are you saying you'd rather I'd left you here alone?''

''If I were wise, I would.'' For the first time, she looked directly at him and he saw that her eyes were heavy with unshed tears. ''We said our final goodbyes this morning, Max, and I don't know that I can weather having to go through doing that again.''

''What if I'm asking you to forget what we said and did this morning, and start out over again with a clean slate?''

She sighed so deeply, her entire body quivered. ''And what if, next week, or next month or next year, you change your mind? Again.''

He stretched out his hand and cupped her face. ''I love you, do you hear? Until this morning, I couldn't bring myself to admit that, and I wouldn't be repeating the words now if I didn't know them to be true.''

''Oh, I'd like to believe you!'' she cried. ''Heaven knows, I've waited long enough to hear you say them.''

''So what's the problem?''

She shook her head, looking almost dazed. ''It's…too sudden. Too much to take in all at once. I'm all at sixes and sevens inside.'' She stepped away from him and spread out her hands as if she were warding off an attack. ''I need to be strong enough not to keep settling for less than the absolute best in our marriage. It would be so easy to give in to my feelings, to accept what you're telling me and forget all the deceit and mistrust that's gone before. But I know in my heart that that would be a mistake.''

Once he'd set his sights on a specific goal, he went after it with single-minded concentration and could no more fathom her waffling at this stage of their relationship than he pretended to understand the vagaries of the fashion industry.

''I keep hearing what you don't want, Gabriella,'' he said testily, ''but I wish you'd spell out exactly what it is you'd like to see happen with us, because I'm at a loss to figure it out.''

She brushed her fingertips under her eyes and made an obvious effort to put her thoughts into some sort of rational order. ''This morning, you asked me why I didn't just let that child take the car, and I said—''

*Some child!* he was tempted to snap, but decided he'd be better off sticking to the real issue. ''I know what you said. I assumed it was shock that had you talking such tripe.''

''Not entirely. The thing is, Max, I really wasn't all that afraid when I realized the danger I was in—no more than usual, that is. Because I'm afraid all the time, and have been ever since I married you. And I'm tired of it.''

''You're comparing being married to me with being held at knifepoint?'' He rolled his eyes disbelievingly. ''That's absurd!''

''No, it isn't. I want to be free to love you unreservedly and be confident you're giving the same back to me. I need to know that if I make a mistake, you'll forgive me. I want to be able to open a letter from you and not be terrified you're writing to tell me you've met someone else and want a divorce. When I hear your voice on the phone, I want to be filled with joy and excitement, instead of dread.''

"Hell, Gabriella, if you're asking for a guarantee that we're never going to disagree again, or make any more mistakes, I can't give you one. Marriage doesn't come with that kind of warranty.''

"I know," she said. "But love does. At least, it should, if it's the kind that's going to last.''

He eyed her suspiciously. "Exactly what are you getting at?''

"I want you to leave for Whistler in the morning and be with your clients. And I'm going to fly to Tokyo on Monday as planned, and from there to Sydney, Milan, Paris, and every other city on my schedule.''

"And then what?''

"I'm not looking any further ahead than that.''

She was making no damned sense and he could have shaken her! Even more, he wanted to put an end to all this *talk* about love, and *show* her what it was all about with actions that spoke more potently than words. "Are you saying we might be through?''

"I hope we're not. I hope what we've found is strong enough to withstand time and distance, but I know the only way I can be sure is to put it to the test.''

The anger came surging out of nowhere, taking him by surprise almost as much as it did her. "And this is your idea of a solution? To walk out on me again? Well, forget it, Gabriella! Either you stay and we work things out together, or we call it quits once and for all.''

"That's blackmail, Max, and you know it," she told him calmly.

"Call it what the devil you like," he seethed. "Those are my terms. Take them or leave them, because I won't be left here twisting in the wind while you go gallivanting

around the world in search of the Holy Grail of matri-
mony!''

"Is that your final word on the subject?"

"It is."

She looked at him long and solemnly, and it seemed
an eternity before she replied, "And you wonder why I'm
afraid of you!"

Then she left the room, climbed the stairs, and very
quietly closed the door to the master suite. It didn't take
a rocket scientist to figure out she wasn't coming out
again, or that he wasn't welcome to join her.

It was back to the guest room for him. The only difference was, this time she was the one who made that
decision.

# CHAPTER ELEVEN

PARIS in late September was lovely that year. Mellow and golden, with the sky behind Notre Dame cathedral a deep restful blue, and the trees along the Champs-Élysées just beginning to turn.

The hotel in Arrondissement 8, where she always stayed, remained as elegantly charming as ever. Her fashion shoots at the various couturier establishments had been a smashing success; a recently completed television interview well received.

Every day, she walked through the Tuileries gardens, or along the banks of the Seine. She took her morning café au lait at her favorite sidewalk bistro, dined often with associates and friends at one or other of the many legendary restaurants in the city. And as she had every night since she'd left him, she came back to her hotel, praying that Max might have called.

It had not happened once in the two months since she'd left, and she was afraid it never would. Still, as she turned on to Avenue George V late on the fourth Tuesday since her return to Paris, and entered the lovely Art Deco vestibule of her hotel, her hopes lifted, only to be dashed when the night clerk, anticipating her question, shook his head sympathetically. "I'm sorry, *madame*. There are no messages."

Dejectedly, she crossed to the elevator and as the ornate brass doors rolled closed behind her and the car began its slow ascent, she leaned her head against the marble wall and wondered for the hundredth time if she'd made the right decision. Should she have stayed in Vancouver? Or would submitting to Max's ultimatum merely have compounded the doubts already besetting her?

The answer was plain enough. If he could let her go so easily, how real was his professed love?

The elevator whispered to a stop on the fifth floor. Listlessly, she stepped out and made her way down the hall to her suite. It was after ten already. The Do Not Disturb sign hung on the door, which meant the maid had already stopped by.

Indeed, she'd left a lamp burning in the tiny entrance hall and even replaced that morning's still-fresh flower arrangement with a huge bouquet of yellow roses sprinkled with starlike baby's breath. Their heady scent filled the small suite.

Gabriella dropped her handbag by the door, kicked off her shoes and wiggled her toes in the thick carpet with a sigh of pleasure. A model's feet took more than their fair share of punishment in the course of a working day. Her shoulders, too. The muscles at the back of her neck felt as if they'd been stitched in place with piano wire.

She would take a long, relaxing bath, maybe order a nightcap of hot milk from room service, spike it with cognac from the bar in the little sitting room—and hope the combination would be enough to induce a sleep deep enough that Max wouldn't find his way into her dreams.

Slipping out of her linen jacket and unbuttoning her blouse, she turned toward the bedroom. At the bureau, she stopped to step out of her skirt, and balanced first on one leg, then the other, to peel off her silk stockings. Finally, clad only in a peach satin camisole and panties, she went to unlatch the tall, narrow windows and let in the sweet night air.

Just as she turned the handle and pushed open the first

pane, the bedside lamp clicked on. "Not that I don't appreciate the striptease, my love, but I can't say I care to have half of Paris horning in on it, too."

The words, laced with amusement, floated from the other end of the room and surely, if there hadn't been a waist-high wrought-iron grille between her and the outside, she'd have pitched forward and fallen five floors to her death on the avenue below.

Clutching the velvet drapery, she fought to control the wild fluttering of her heart. "Well, I'm not quite finished yet," she said breathlessly. "I'm saving the best part for last and intend it to be a very private viewing."

She dared to turn then, and meet his gaze. He lay stretched out on the bed, feet crossed at the ankles, hands linked behind his head. He needed a shave, his clothes were travel-wrinkled, his hair a mess, and he looked so utterly gorgeous that she went weak at the knees.

"Hello, Max," she said.

"Hi, sweetheart."

There weren't sparks flying through the air, but there should have been. The atmosphere was so rarefied her lungs could barely function.

She wished she could think of something memorable to say, something she and Max would look back on in their dotage and laugh about. She wished she could find the courage to run to him; to feel his arms close around her and know that, this time, she'd finally come home to stay, even though she was half a world away from Vancouver.

Instead, she simply stared—at his beautiful, sexy mouth, his serious, summer-blue eyes, his wonderful, unforgettable face. And because she was a dolt who never could keep herself together where he was concerned, she did what she always did when the feelings grew too intense to bear. She started to cry.

For once, it was the right thing to do. He leaped off the bed and was at her side in a single bound. "You dope!" he growled. "I'm never letting you out of my sight again. Do you always just walk into your hotel room and start undressing, without first checking to make sure the place is secure?"

"Don't yell at me!" she sobbed.

"Why not? It's what I seem to do best."

But he wasn't yelling, not at all. His voice was flowing over her like warm honey laced with deep, dark chocolate. His hands were stroking over her skin and leaving trails of tenderness in their wake. He was murmuring magical healing words; calling her his darling, his very own beloved. And telling her he'd missed her so badly he'd damn near gone mad.

"I'm such an ass," he said. "A permanent work-in-progress. I don't know how you're ever going to train me to behave. But I hope you'll at least give it a try. Because I need you, my Gabriella, and I'm sorry if it's too soon for you to hear this, but I just don't think I can go another day without you."

"I thought you'd given up on us," she said, still sniffling like a baby. "I really didn't think—"

"On me, perhaps, but never on you. I've gone through a living hell these last two months but it was worth it if, at the end of it all, we're together again. It took me a long time to face up to the fact that each time you left me, I drove you to it, and even longer for me to admit how badly I missed you, or how empty my life was without you in it. So I decided that instead of hoping you'd have the good sense to come back to me, I'd do better by coming to you for a change and throwing myself on your mercy.''

He looked at her searchingly. "Have I left it too late, Gabriella? Is the kind of glamorous life you lead here more appealing than being plain Mrs. Max Logan? Do I have to follow you all over the world in order to stay close to you?''

"There was a time when you'd have run anywhere in the world, just to get away from me," she reminded him. "Have you forgotten what an unwilling bridegroom you were?''

"No. But I know now that we'd have ended up at the altar sooner or later. It just came sooner than I was ready to accept it, that's all. But I'm ready now, Gabriella, and not so proud or stubborn that I won't get down on my knees and beg for another chance, if that's what it'll take.''

"If you'd kiss me," she said, melting against him, "I think I might be persuaded to dispense with the groveling and settle in favor of being plain Mrs. Max Logan.''

He didn't need a second invitation. His lips closed over hers with such sureness and passion that all the dark, terrible doubts she'd entertained over the last two months— the last two years—finally sank into oblivion.

It seemed the most natural thing in the world for him to take her to bed in that elegant Parisian hotel room. For them to renew their vows to one another in the most romantic city in the world. For him to bring her to the edge of insanity and tell her he loved her as they fell together into that deep, thrilling chasm of release.

But the truly remarkable thing was that they could just as well have been in a hut in the Himalayas, or a tent in the Sahara, because what made it unique and glorious was the trust they'd forged from all the tears and misery—not just in the moment but in tomorrow and all the long, lovely years that stretched ahead.

*Together for the first time
in one Collector's Edition!*

**New York Times bestselling authors**

# Barbara Delinsky

# Catherine Coulter

# Linda Howard

# Forever Yours

**A special trade-size volume containing three
complete novels that showcase the passion,
imagination and stunning power that these
talented authors are famous for.**

Coming to your favorite retail outlet in December 2001.

**HARLEQUIN®**
*Makes any time special* ®

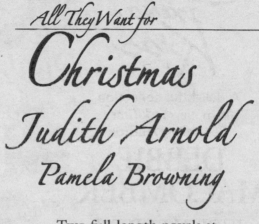

# WITH HARLEQUIN AND SILHOUETTE

## There's a romance to fit your every mood.

### Passion

Harlequin Temptation

Harlequin Presents

Silhouette Desire

### Pure Romance

Harlequin Romance

Silhouette Romance

### Home & Family

Harlequin
American Romance

Silhouette
Special Edition

### A Longer Story With More

Harlequin
Superromance

### Suspense & Adventure

Harlequin Intrigue

Silhouette Intimate
Moments

### Humor

Harlequin Duets

### Historical

Harlequin Historicals

### Special Releases

Other great
romances
to explore